$2.00

The Deadliest Shot in Denver

"Now!"

The word was barely off the youngster's lips before Longarm's big Colt bellowed, and the head-sized rock sprayed lead and stone chips.

The boys blinked. Neither of them had yet touched the grips of his gun. Only the one who had called the start signal had reached toward his pistol.

"Now that I have your attention," Longarm said softly, "let's you and me talk."

TABOR EVANS

LONGARM

AND THE HANGMAN'S NOOSE

JOVE BOOKS, NEW YORK

LONGARM AND THE HANGMAN'S NOOSE

A Jove Book / published by arrangement with
the author

PRINTING HISTORY
Jove edition / May 1989

ISBN: 0-515-10015-3

Jove books are published by The Berkley Publishing Group,
200 Madison Avenue, New York, New York 10016.
The name "JOVE" and the "J" logo
are trademarks belonging to Jove Publications, Inc.

PRINTED IN THE UNITED STATES OF AMERICA

10 9 8 7 6 5 4 3 2 1

Chapter 1

Longarm was the first passenger off the train. Before the coach had finished squealing and lurching to rest he had brushed past the conductor, hopped over the steel steps that were not yet unfolded, and jumped down to the platform.

The telegraphed message had said the robbery was in progress even as the wire was being transmitted. Probably everything was over and done with by now—after all, Englewood was a good twenty-five minutes from Denver by rail—but there was always a possibility that something could still be happening. If the tall, narrow-hipped U.S. deputy marshal missed the gang it would not be for lack of trying.

The United States Post Office in Englewood was only a block and a half from the railroad station. Long-arm made the distance in a long, loping run.

He slowed to a walk as he neared the front of the post office.

He was too late, as he could readily see from the number of local cops milling uncertainly on the sidewalk . . . and from the ambulance that was drawn up beside the hitch rail in front of the building.

The ambulance driver was having difficulty calming his team of light, quick horses, which meant the ambulance must have arrived only moments ahead of Long-arm. Already, though, the rear doors of the rig had been thrown open, and the attendants were somewhere inside the post office.

The presence of the ambulance was not good. The telegram had said nothing about injuries.

1

An Englewood policeman in a blue coat and black-brimmed blue cap tried to block Longarm's entry to the post office. A flash of his badge took care of that.

The post office building was small, and at the moment it was overly crowded. Police officers and a postal clerk stood gawking while a pair of ambulance attendants tried to tend to two patients at once.

On the floor beside the little gate that blocked entry to the pigeonholes and working area behind the counter there was a man with a bloody shirtfront. Longarm recognized the victim. He was Mack Bowen, postmaster here and a political crony of some of Denver's leading citizens.

Slumped against the wall beneath a pinboard display of Wanted posters there was a pale woman. The second attendant was holding a vial of smelling salts under her nose and trying to bring her out of her vapors.

The woman obviously hadn't really been hurt, though, Longarm saw. He knelt at Bowen's side and raised a questioning eyebrow to the man who was trying to fix a compress bandage over a small, bubbling hole in Bowen's chest.

"Lungs," the attendant said crisply. "One bullet." He did not add that it was still too early to know if Mack Bowen would live or die. But then, he did not have to. Longarm had seen wounds like this more often than he might have wished. There was just no way to judge the ultimate outcome. Not yet. The human body can be amazingly resilient—or roll over and expire from a comparative scratch. Longarm had seen it happen both ways.

He took a closer look at Bowen. The postmaster was having trouble drawing breath, but his color looked good. He had a fighting chance to make it if his will to live was strong. Longarm nodded to the attendant and stepped over Bowen's legs so he could go behind the counter.

2

The officer in charge of the local investigation was a man Longarm had seen before but never actually met.

"Long, isn't it?" the cop asked.

Longarm nodded and extended a hand.

"I'm Joe Doyle, day sergeant here." He shook Longarm's hand. "Pleasure to meet you, Marshal. You got onto it quick."

"Someone had sense enough to get a wire off while it was still in progress. But I sure don't have much in the way of details."

Doyle nodded and drew Longarm aside. In a low, calm voice he said, "The clerk there is Albert Tyrel. I expect you know Mr. Bowen."

"Uh-huh."

"Bowen and Tyrel were both behind the counter when the robbers came in. There were six of them, all wearing dusters and with feed sacks over their heads as masks. Cutouts for eye holes and like that. Jeans, high-heeled boots and spurs showing under the dusters. Cowboys, more'n likely. Two of the gang stayed outside holding the horses. Nondescript browns, by the way. No one noticed the brands, if there were any.

"Anyhow, four of them came inside and pulled revolvers. They demanded the cash from the drawers and the mailbag that was supposed to go out on the 12:17 to Denver."

Longarm glanced at the clock on the front wall. It was now 12:09.

"Normal schedule," Doyle said, the policeman obviously anticipating Longarm's question. "Incoming should be on the train that I assume you just got off. Outgoing runs on the turnaround. They follow the same schedule six days each week."

Longarm nodded his thanks.

"Anyhow, the robbers came in and made the demand, and the leader of them started for the gate there. Bowen moved to step in front of him. Tyrel doesn't know what Bowen intended. To try and stop them or say

3

something or, hell, open the gate for him. Whatever, the leader of the gang didn't bother to tell Mack to get out of the way or say another word. He up with his gun and blows one square into Mack's chest from a distance of four or five feet. Then he comes behind the counter and goes for the mailbag that Tyrel had just closed but hadn't locked yet.

"While he's doing that two more of them come behind the counter and rifle the cash drawers. They brought little sacks with them to dump everything into. They took the money, stamps, blank money orders, date stamps, gum bands, every damn thing they could put a hand on. Dumped drawers and everything into their bags.

"While that's going on, the one on the other side of the counter is getting tired of listening to that lady out there scream . . . she was the only customer in the place at the time, was writing out a penny postcard on the counter there . . . so he pokes her in the titty with the barrel of his revolver, and she faints dead away."

Longarm grunted. He was sure the experience was rough on the woman, but there were worse things that could have happened. She could ask Mack Bowen if she didn't believe it.

Doyle turned to Tyrel and beckoned the clerk to join them. "Tell the marshal here about the gun Mack was shot with."

"What kind of marshal are you?" Tyrel asked, looking Long up and down.

What the man saw was imposing enough. Longarm was well over six feet tall, narrow in the waist but broad through the shoulders. He had brown hair, a sweeping brown mustache and gray, piercing eyes. He wore a tweed coat and corduroy trousers, black stovepipe boots and a flat-crowned brown Stetson. Mostly, though, seen from a criminal's perspective, he wore a double-action Colt Thunderer in a cross-draw holster just to the left of his belt buckle.

"I'm federal," Longarm explained. He added, "Just like you," to ease the postal clerk's obvious skepticism about talking to a stranger.

Tyrel nodded. "The gun was an old Navy Colt," he said. "Converted to handle cartridges, which would make it a .38."

"You're sure about that?" Back during the recent unpleasantness, the Navy Colt in .36 cap-and-ball had been arguably the best handgun available in the world. It had enjoyed a period of well-earned popularity that quickly faded once metallic cartridge arms became readily available in the postwar years. The cap-and-ball Colts would have died years sooner except for patent rights owned by the makers of inferior revolvers. A good many of the old Colts were converted to use cartridges at the time—the gunsmith conversion efforts avoided patent infringement claims because the updated versions were being modified and not manufactured as cartridge arms—but such guns had become a rarity during the past decade. Longarm doubted he had seen one in actual, everyday use in six, eight years, which was why he questioned Tyrel's identification.

"Marshal Long, I may be only a postal clerk, and small potatoes to a man like you, but I used to be a cavalryman once upon a time, and I know a Navy Colt when I see one. I carried four of them myself, two holstered and two on the saddle. And if there'd been such a thing then as the cartridge conversion, I'd've damn sure paid to have mine made over. You can tell the difference easy, what with the fluted cylinder and the loading gate and the ball ram being missing from under the barrel."

Longarm looked back at Doyle. "You're making a lot of the identification of this gun. I take it you have a reason?"

"Evidence, Longarm. When you arrest the guy that shot Mack."

Longarm raised an eyebrow.

"We as good as have an identification," Doyle said,

5

"which is what I've been getting around to here. But you'll want some physical evidence to back it up since there was a feed sack over his face."

"You don't have him in custody, then?"

Doyle shook his head. "The robbers took off at a dead run south of town along the railroad tracks. They were riding in the ballast so there aren't any prints to follow. And o' course in town here, well, there just aren't that many saddle horses handy. By the time we could have got a posse mounted, the robbers were long gone. But I know where you can find the leader of them, anyway. I expect you can work on him to identify the rest of them."

"Who . . . ?"

"Longarm, it was 'Big' Little that held up the post office here and shot Mack Bowen down in cold blood."

"No!" Longarm blurted before he had time to think. "It couldn't have been Big."

"I swear to you that it was, Longarm. I'm sure of it."

Longarm sighed. He had never met anyone, at least no one who knew the man, who did not immediately and thoroughly like Chester "Big" Little.

And Custis Long was no exception to that rule, damnit.

"Tell me about it," Longarm said unhappily.

Chapter 2

The man who shot Mack Bowen down was exceptionally tall. Six-foot-seven or -eight. He wore high-heeled
boots with narrow toes, spurs with huge Mexican
rowels, a battered hat in the four-pinch Montana peak
style, and walked with a decided limp, his left leg being
stiff.

Inconspicuous he was not.

"Damn," Longarm said.

"I guess I don't have to ask if you know Big," Joe
Doyle said. "And I got to admit, Longarm, I feel the
same way. But there just can't be much doubt about
who did it. Hell, Longarm, he even mounted his horse
from the right side after he shot Mack and run outside.
If you know Big you know as well as I do that that's
how he has to mount. His left leg won't bend for him to
get on a horse from the proper side, so he's gotta use the
off side and mount like an Injun."

Longarm nodded unhappily.

The rest of it fit too, damnit. The narrow-toed boots
when most men wore pouchlike boots with rounded
toes. The high, Montana crimp in the hat. The Mexican
spurs with the oversized rowels. Everything.

Damnit, anyway, it all added up to Big Little.

"I like the guy too," Doyle said softly. "Not that it
makes any difference."

Albert Tyrel scowled. "If this is the kind of justice
Mr. Bowen can expect from you two . . ."

"We don't like it," Longarm informed him. "That
doesn't mean we won't do our jobs, Mr. Tyrel. I take it
you don't know Big?"

"Don't and don't want to," Tyrel snapped. "I never saw the man before, and quite frankly I don't want to see him again. The way he walked in here and just shot poor Mr. Bowen down, it was terrible. There was no need for it, you see. Mr. Bowen wasn't even armed. He couldn't have defended himself if he'd tried. Not that this Little friend of yours gave him any chance to, mind. Just shot him down. Why, I wouldn't treat a rabid dog so poorly."

"Yes, sir," Longarm said.

On the other side of the gate the attendants had the woman on her feet now and were busy carrying Bowen out to the waiting ambulance.

Longarm and Joe Doyle moved out to the lobby area now that there was more room there and braced the matronly postal patron with first sympathy and then some questions.

The woman—she was a Mrs. Frake—was still shaken, but lucid enough now that the initial shock had worn off.

Her story was very much the same as that given by Tyrel.

The robbers came inside. The one in front was huge. A real bear of a man with broad shoulders and a big hat and a feed sack over his face. He walked with a limp. She could not remember which leg he limped with. She remembered his gun well enough. No, she had no idea what *kind* it was. After all, all guns look alike anyway. This one was big and black and it frightened her.

And then the big man shot Mr. Bowen, and yes, she remembered that she screamed and the other man who was close to her wanted her to stop, and she really did try to stop screaming but she couldn't.

And then that awful man, who also had a simply huge pistol, pointed it at her and actually *touched* her with it—she didn't specify precisely *where* he touched her—and then everything went fuzzy, and the next thing she knew she was sitting against the wall and an-

8

other man, a nice man, was trying to revive her, and now she was trembling and did not feel at *all* well, thank you, and would Officer Doyle please have one of his officers escort her home right *now*, thank you, because if she didn't get inside her own house and lock her doors and have a cup of tea she was going to be sick, she *knew* she was.

Doyle summoned a blue-coated officer and had him take Mrs. Frake home.

"I better get over to the clinic," Doyle said. "There's going to be hell to pay around here with Mack Bowen being shot. Likely in Denver, too. Mack has some mighty powerful friends, you know. They're gonna want a quick arrest and a quicker hanging after this one."

"Don't I know it," Longarm said. "But I just can't believe . . ."

"Believe it," Doyle insisted. He hesitated. "Look, d'you want me to go out and make the arrest? I mean, it did happen in my jurisdiction."

"No." Longarm smiled. "I thank you for the offer, but it's a federal case. Theft from the mails and assault on a government employee. That makes it mine. But I appreciate the offer."

"Tell you the truth, Longarm, I was hoping you'd say that. Big comes to Englewood once a month or so to do some drinking. Nicest, happiest fellow I ever met. I sure always enjoyed talking with him. Sure did like the guy."

"Me too."

"Hey, you two. Are you going to kiss the son of a bitch or arrest him?" Tyrel put in.

Joe Doyle gave the postal clerk a dark look, and Tyrel shut up.

"I expect I'm going to have to hire a horse and mosey over to the Circle Y," Longarm said. "Any suggestions?"

"There's a place on the way to the clinic. I'll take you by there," Doyle offered.

"Thanks." To Tyrel he added, "I'd like you to make up a list of everything that was stolen. Everything you can think of. And if you can recall who was in with outgoing mail this morning, I'd like you to ask them what was in their letters or parcels. Not what they said, of course, but if there was anything of value going out like cash or money orders or whatever. Can you do that?"

Tyrel looked sullen.

"It would help with the prosecution if we can recover any physical evidence and prove it was taken at the same time Mr. Bowen was shot," Longarm explained.

"I'll do it," Tyrel conceded, the explanation apparently making a difference.

"Get your list together over the next few days. Everything you can think of or your customers can. I'll stop by and pick it up later."

Tyrel nodded.

Longarm followed Doyle outside. There were some gawkers in the street but not many now that the ambulance was gone and things inside the post office could return to normal.

The livery was three blocks away. The ride to the Circle Y where Big Little worked would take no more than an hour or so.

Longarm was not really looking forward to what he had to do this afternoon. He almost wished he had accepted Joe Doyle's offer to handle the arrest.

Chapter 3

The Circle Y ranch was south of Denver and pretty much due east from Englewood. Longarm had been there a few times before. The place was fairly close to the Diamond K on Cherry Creek.

Actually, calling the Circle Y a ranch was misleading. The term was more honorary than earned, at least under the popular conception of what a ranch should be.

The word "ranch" implies vast acreages of grazing land dotted liberally with livestock. And the Circle Y was nothing remotely like that.

Longarm had no idea how much land Circle Y owner Pat Vieren held title to, but if he had to guess he would peg it in the neighborhood of a hundred acres, more or less. And unless Vieren's wife, Althea, had bought herself a milch cow since the last time Longarm was by, there wasn't a cow or steer on the place.

The Circle Y was a highly specialized horse operation. And not just any horses either. Pat Vieren specialized in high-quality stallions. The Circle Y was a stud farm, offering breeding service to outside mares for a fee, and providing a selection of studs from which the mare owners could choose. The Vieren studs included a rangy, long-legged Tennessee plantation walker, a close-coupled and cat-quick cutting horse, a snake-necked thoroughbred better than anything the army's Remount Service would ever see, a mammoth full-blooded Percheron, and several others. All in all, there was something on the place to meet nearly any breeder's specialized needs.

Vieren had a very few fancy mares of his own that he

11

used to produce his future stallions, but basically the man made his living on the strength of his studs' performance.

That, in fact, was what had brought Longarm to his barns now and again. Like many other Denver area outfits, the boys at the Diamond K liked to go to Pat Vieren first when they were looking for a stallion to put to a favored mare, or wanted to make a purchase on those rare occasions when Vieren announced a sale of unwanted fillies from his spring get. Longarm had ridden along with friends a time or two simply out of admiration for the quality of horseflesh he would see there.

So he knew how to find the Circle Y. Damnit.

He made good time cutting straight across country to the stud farm and avoiding the mostly north-south roads that extended from Denver down toward Castle Rock and Palmer Lake. It was midafternoon when he rode into the yard at the Circle Y.

Vieren had a tight, well-maintained little outfit.

A comfortable house had been built in the shelter of a copse of cottonwoods. Behind it were lines of exceptionally sturdy stud stalls, each a separate structure of its own with a high-fenced run attached so the often nervous and flighty stallions could find sun or shelter as they pleased.

Equipment sheds, breaking pens, a breeding chute and more were scattered over the property. Vieren's mares occupied a small pasture on the east side of the property close to a handful of covered birthing pens. That end of the property was dominated by a huge hay barn. Vieren did not own land enough to provide graze for his animals, and in any event would have wanted to keep the stallions separated and under close supervision. He had to buy many tons of hay each year to feed his stock.

The place seemed deserted when Longarm rode into the yard and tied his rented gelding at a hitch rail.

"Hello?"

There was no response. He tried knocking on the house door without result, though the unlocked and unlatched door swung open at his touch. He called inside, then pulled the door to and set the latch lest the wind blow it open again.

Muttering, Longarm pulled out a cheroot and lighted it. He wondered if he should check inside the house and see if Pat and his missus were all right. If Big had for some reason gone round the bend . . .

"Longarm!"

He looked across the yard. Big Little was standing in the doorway of one of the stud shelters with a pitchfork in his huge hands.

Big was grinning and waving. He acted like nothing at all untoward had ever happened.

Longarm clamped the end of the cheroot between his teeth and crossed the yard to the man.

Big was damn well named. At least his nickname fit. The rest of it certainly did not.

Big towered three or four inches above Longarm's own considerable height and probably outweighed the marshal by a hundred pounds or more.

Big as Big was, there was not a scrap of fat evident anywhere on him. He had the shoulders of a half-grown ox, a chest like a beer barrel, and muscles like tempered steel. The hardness of his body, though, was balanced somewhat by an undeniable softness between the ears. Big Little had body enough to accommodate two strong men, but his mind was forever that of a ten-year-old boy. He was like a great, *gallumphing*, overgrown puppy. Happy and uncoordinated. Friendly and ever eager to please.

"Hi, Longarm." Big grinned at his friend—but, hell, everyone was Big's friend—and set the points of the pitchfork tines onto the earth so he could fold his wrists over the handle and lean on it.

"How are you doin' today, Big?"

"Just fine, thank you." He was still grinning.

13

"Working hard?"

"You bet." He took the idle question seriously and proceeded to show his friend exactly what he had been doing when Longarm arrived.

He motioned Longarm inside the small, tightly built stud barn and pointed with no small degree of pride to the floor, which was covered nearly a foot deep in freshly laid, sweet-smelling straw. A loaded manure spreader was parked by the gate nearby.

"This place here b'longs to Tartan Hi Boy. He's out visitin' a mare t'day, so while the place is empty I'm giving it a good cleaning." The grin got wider. "Nice, huh?"

"Very nice," Longarm assured him. Longarm remained at the doorway, not wanting to enter another man's barn with a lighted cheroot. A fallen ash in the fresh straw could spell disaster. And the presence of a lighted cigar or cigarette or even pipe inside a straw- or hay-filled barn could make a visitor damned well unwelcome whether or not an accident occurred.

Big tripped over something, possibly his own huge feet, and kicked a bare patch in the newly laid straw. Patiently he used the pitchfork to rearrange the straw so the surface was smooth and the bed thick in readiness for the return of Tartan Hi Boy.

Hi Boy, Longarm thought he remembered, was the Vieren Percheron stallion. Although just where a horse with French origins would get a Scots name was anybody's guess. Maybe it was the Clyde that was Tartan Hi Boy.

"So Hi Boy's gone visiting, huh?"

"Yeah," Big said happily. "Mr. Heath sent his oldest boy over last night to tell us his mare was comin' in season, so this mornin' Tom hitched Hi Boy t' the stud cart an' drove him over there."

Longarm nodded. Tom was Tom Lee, Pat Vieren's other hired hand. Longarm didn't know Heath, but he

14

understood well enough what Tom and the man would be doing today.

Mares are flighty when they are in season ready for breeding, and it can be difficult under the best of circumstances to get them to accept a stud, and then once accepted to produce a full-term foal as a result of the mating. Because travel can put stress on a newly impregnated mare and cause her to lose her fetus, common custom was for the stallion to be driven to wherever the mare was and the breeding take place at the mare owner's place.

The stud cart was a logical outgrowth of that practice. It is easier for a stallion to walk than be hauled for service, and most breeders of Vieren's quality used stud carts for that purpose.

A stud cart is a plain and exceptionally sturdy two-wheeled cart that the stud handler can ride while the stud in question transports itself for the breeding to come.

Not only does the cart allow the stallion to travel, after a very few uses it also prepares the stallion for the breeding. Horses are basically stupid animals, but they do have phenomenal memories. After one or two uses, a stallion quickly learns that when he is hitched to the stud cart—usually used for no other purpose—it means he is on his way to a mare. It gets him excited and horny in anticipation of the mating.

Longarm held his cheroot at arm's length outside Tartan Hi Boy's shelter and tapped the ash onto bare ground.

"Where're Pat and Althea?" he asked.

"Gone to town," Big said. He propped the handle of the pitchfork against his chest and began to examine the ball of his thumb for a splinter.

"Did they say when they'd be back?"

"Don't remember." Big frowned in concentration. "I don't think they did, Longarm. D'you want me to give them a message?"

15

"No, I don't think so." Longarm took another pull on his cheroot and held the smoke deep in his lungs while he dropped the butt and carefully ground it out under his boot toe. "Something I was wanting to ask you, Big."

"Yeah?"

"I've been looking for a Navy Colt revolver. Somebody told me you might have one."

Big laughed. "A gun? Me? Longarm, I never owned a gun in my life. Somebody was funning you, Longarm."

"Maybe. You don't have a Navy Colt though?"

"Aw shucks, Longarm. I got no use for a gun. They're only t' hurt things with. I don't want t' hurt nuthin'." That line of thought, probably having to do with things that were hurt, somehow translated itself inside Big's brain to something else, and he straightened with a wide smile and beamed at his friend. "Want t' see something purty, Longarm?"

"Sure I do, Big."

Big leaned the pitchfork in a corner of Tartan Hi Boy's stall and motioned for Longarm to follow. They walked toward the mare pasture, Longarm trailing behind Big's awkward, limping gait, and then angled toward the birthing pens, unused at this time of year.

With a show of growing excitement Big drew the bolt on a door and swung it wide. "Watch your head," he warned. He had to duck to enter the building. Longarm had no need to. "See?" He pointed with considerable pride to a weanling filly standing in a shadowy corner.

The filly nickered softly when Big came in. She scampered to his side and nuzzled his palm as if searching there for a tidbit. Big stroked her neck gently and reached into his pocket for a scrap of carrot that he fed her.

When the filly moved, Longarm noticed that her off foreleg was crooked. She moved well enough, but there was a decided twist to the stick-thin leg.

16

"She's mine, Longarm." Big grinned. "Ain't she purty?"

"She sure is, Big."

It was true. The weanling was a scruffy black and brown color now, but it was possible to see that beneath her foal coat she had patches of lighter coloring already beginning to show. Eventually she would slick off and turn into a buckskin with a blaze and snip and a handsome set to her delicate head.

"Mr. Pat was gonna knock her in the head when he seen that leg, Longarm. Can you imagine that?"

Longarm could imagine it, but he held his tongue.

"He let me have her instead."

"What are you going to do about the leg, Big?"

"She won't grow out o' it on her own, but I c'n correct it, I think. Soon as her hoofs are quit bein' so soft I'll build her a little shoe. A corrective shoe, like. Get her t' shiftin' her weight so the leg turns. See?"

He picked up the little filly's hoof and sketched quickly in the air with his big, awkward fingers to show Longarm how he intended to build the shoe and cause the leg to grow out straight.

"Way I figure it, Longarm, I c'n get it straight enough that she'll be usable long as I make her shoes special. An' I swear she's just the purtiest thing I ever seen."

He grinned with pride as he set the twisted leg gently back to the ground and petted the little horse. The filly pressed tight against him and nibbled at the edge of Big's pocket with mobile, hairy little lips. He laughed and produced another bit of carrot to feed her.

Longarm frowned.

Damnit to hell anyway. How was he supposed to believe that this Chester Little was the same man who a few hours ago pointed a gun point-blank into the chest of Mack Bowen and shot the postmaster down in cold blood?

17

Now just how in hell was he supposed to believe that?

"You say you've been here working on that stall ever since Tom and Pat left, Big?"

"Didn' I do a nice job? Smells s'nice in there now. Soon as Tartan Hi Boy gets home I'll give him a nice bath an' he'll smell as nice as his place does," Big said. He seemed genuinely happy that the big horse would be comfortable.

Nice. Big was awfully fond of the word. Well, dammit, *Big* was nice.

He was a genuinely nice man. Gentle and slow and truly concerned for the welfare of the horses he loved.

How the hell could a man like that shoot Mack Bowen in the chest?

The facts back in Englewood seemed plain enough, all right.

But the facts here at the Circle Y were just about as opposite from them as any two sets of facts would ever likely get.

Now that was the simple truth of the matter, Longarm thought.

Besides, his gut instinct told him that Big Little was not the man he wanted. No son of a bitch could stand here and talk with Big and see him play with his filly and believe that Big shot the postmaster. Nobody.

"Fuck it," Longarm said. His voice was sharp and angry, although he wasn't entirely sure if it was Big he was angry with or himself.

"Par'n me?"

Longarm didn't answer.

"D'you say something, Longarm?"

"Nothing important, Big."

"Oh." The confusion that had for a moment clouded Big's broad, innocent face cleared, and he grinned again.

Longarm turned away. "I better go now, Big. I have work to do."

18

"You want I should tell Mr. Pat anything for you, Longarm?"

"No, Big. No messages, thanks."

"I'm sure glad you come by, Longarm." He gave the filly a final pat and followed Longarm out, carefully closing and latching the door behind him before he limped beside Longarm toward the rented horse. "Next time maybe Mr. Pat will be here for you t' talk to. I know I ain't much comp'ny when a man wants t' talk serious," Big added with no trace of displeasure.

"You're all the company anybody could want for, Big," Longarm assured him. "Besides, we're friends, aren't we?"

"You bet," Big said with a wide, happy smile. "Ain't it nice t' have friends?"

"Yes, it surely is," Longarm said seriously. He swung onto the saddle of the rented gelding and smiled at his friend Big Little. "You take care, Big."

"I will, Longarm. I surely will. You have a nice day now, hear?"

"You too, Big."

Longarm wheeled the gelding and rode away from the Circle Y with a grimace.

He was probably going to have to do some tall explaining to Billy Vail. But damnit he just did *not* believe that Chester Little shot Mack Bowen or anybody else. And he was not going to arrest the poor fellow just because somebody else did not share that opinion. And anybody who demanded otherwise, well, the hell with them and all their cousins too. He just couldn't bring himself to do it.

He bumped the horse into a lope and headed not for Englewood but north to Denver.

Chapter 4

Billy Vail was pissed. The United States Marshal for the Denver District was normally a fairly placid man and not much given to paying attention to outside influences. But this time it was not so much the political pressures he objected to as it was the fact that he happened to agree with the local politicians who were expecting Big Little's arrest, and would now be damned well demanding it and probably Custis Long's head on a platter too.

"Damnit, Long. You know better than this."

Longarm was seated in a leather-covered chair in his boss's Federal Building office while Billy paced back and forth in front of him with his arms waving and his normally pink cheeks turning a bright red. Even his bald spot seemed to be glowing.

"You *know* better. You're allowing your personal feelings to intrude on the job. That isn't like you, Deputy. Or at least I didn't *think* it was like you. Are you losing your touch, Custis? Or your damned mind?"

Longarm kept his head down and his mouth shut. There were times when it was okay to crack wise with the boss. This was not one of them.

"We have a positive identification of the gunman. We have a man dead."

Longarm raised his eyes to meet Billy's. Dead. He hadn't heard that. Bowen was still breathing the last time Longarm saw him, when he was being carried out to the ambulance on a litter.

"So what do *you* do? You ride over and have a nice chat with the killer and then come back without him.

And then you have the gall to tell me that *he said you should have a nice day*? Damnit, Longarm, I should *hope* he would think that. You certainly made *his* day nice enough."

Billy puffed up in frustration for a moment, his mouth working helplessly as anger overcame his ability to spit the words out.

"Look, uh, Billy, I..."

"Shut up," Vail snapped. "Just...shut...up. Let me think for a moment."

Billy shook his head.

"Three different delegations," he said when he was able to go on. "Three different visitations, to this office, by leading members of this community. Two state senators. Three state representatives. Two mayors. Two gray little men who represent the most influential people in this entire, sovereign state. They come here. They express concern. And what do I tell them? Stupid me, Deputy. I tell them I have my best man on it and right at that very moment this alleged best man is busy arresting the perpetrator." He paused to gulp for breath again. "Stupid me," he muttered.

"So what happens next, Deputy? You come in here and tell me you failed to put the murderer under arrest. That is what happened next, Deputy. And I refer to you as 'Deputy' as a temporary courtesy, Deputy Long. Is it necessary for me to add that?" He snorted. "Probably. Yes, that probably is necessary. You certainly don't seem able to think anything out for yourself any longer, so I suppose I do have to explain that to you. Shall I draw you pictures, too?"

Longarm stared silently at his hands clasped in his lap.

He'd never seen Billy like this before. Never, no matter how serious a blunder anybody in the office pulled.

And, damnit, Longarm still did not believe that he'd made a mistake with Big Little. No matter what those political hacks claimed, Longarm did not believe he had made a mistake about Big.

As for what Billy thought, well, all Billy had was secondhand information. He hadn't been at the post office any more than Longarm had.

Longarm tried to point that out to the normally rational and calm marshal, but Billy was not much interested in listening to explanations—or even apologies—right at the moment. He wasn't done ranting yet. Longarm clamped his jaw closed again and dropped his eyes. Better to let Billy get it all out of his system.

Apparently there wasn't going to be time enough, though, for the spleens to be vented and the blood let down off the boiling point.

Longarm listened in thorough misery to words like "stupid" and "fatuous" and "pig headed" and then, finally, incredibly, "fired."

He was almost too numb and distressed to realize the full extent of Billy Vail's anger.

He did realize, though, that the next thing he knew for sure was that he was outside the Federal Building, standing on the long-familiar stone steps and looking back.

And the inside coat pocket where he normally carried a stamped steel badge was suddenly empty of the long-familiar weight. The badge that used to be there lay now on the broad, polished surface of the marshal's desk.

Damn, Billy'd been pissed.

Chapter 5

Longarm stopped at Maury's for a drink. The place was right on the way home. And he hadn't anyplace better to go. He still felt numb and more than a little disoriented.

That first drink went down like the glass had been empty to begin with, and he called for another. He still couldn't feel much of anything, so he tried a third.

After that the counting kind of got away from him. There were more. He was pretty sure of that. Just how many, though, he was in no condition to tell.

The next thing he was sure of was a gray half-light outside a window he did not recognize, a window covered by curtains he was pretty sure he'd never seen before, and he decided he was lying in a strange bed somewhere, that it was dawn or close to it, and that he wasn't exactly alone in this unknown bed.

There was a warmth close to his right hip, and the mattress he was lying on—not nearly as lumpy an article as the one in his rented room—had a weight on it that tilted the bed sideways just a little.

Or was it maybe that the world was tilted a little sideways at the moment?

Longarm pondered that question for a while with his eyes closed and eventually decided he would not commit himself on the subject. Maybe the bed was tilted; maybe the world was. Right now it hardly seemed to matter which.

He opened his eyes again and winced. The light was still dim beyond those curtains, but it was bright enough to strengthen the pounding that was battering the inside of his skull.

He closed his eyes again and tried to ignore the sharp, bitter taste of bile on his tongue. He must have thrown up sometime during the night. He couldn't remember doing it. Couldn't smell it either, so he must have been someplace else when it happened. If it happened.

A grown man oughta know better than this, he chided himself. Or be able to handle it if he just had to go and do it.

Longarm forced his eyes open and tried to sit upright. That was a mistake. His head throbbed, and the room spun crazily around him. He lay back, closed his eyes and permitted himself a groan.

"Good morning, honey." The voice was soft and sweetly feminine. An angel's voice, beside his right ear.

Except it couldn't be an angel, damnit. No angel would want to have anything to do with him right now.

He groaned again.

The angel voice chuckled. "Take your time, honey."

Longarm swallowed, fighting back an impulse to puke up whatever was left from last night's debauchery, and kept his eyes squeezed tightly shut. The room still spun but not quite so badly while his eyes were shut.

"I know what will help you, honey," the angel voice said. "Just lay still now."

The advice was unnecessary. He wasn't going anywhere.

Longarm felt the covers being pulled back off of him —until he felt them taken away he hadn't realized they had been there—and then a warm, engulfing presence somewhere south of where his belt should have been, if he'd been wearing one.

Apparently he was naked. He hadn't realized that either. But this hardly seemed a good time to wonder where his clothes had gotten to.

"You surely are good, honey," the angel voice said. "You do know how to make a girl feel good. Now I can

24

repay the favor." The angel voice chuckled again. The sound of it was warm and friendly.

Except it sure as hell was no angel making those sounds.

No angel would be doing *that* to a human. Huh-*uh*!

Something—he couldn't tell what, exactly, but something mighty nice indeed—closed warm and wet and soft and deep around his morning hard-on.

Mmm-mmm-*mmm*!

Oh, my.

Longarm kept his eyes shut and tried to relax and concentrate on a certain few selected feelings.

The angel voice was right about one thing, though. The things that were happening down there sure did take his mind off everything else. His head wasn't pounding so bad anymore, and the world seemed to have quit twirling.

The wet-warm, soft-deep sensations continued. A little quicker now. A little more insistent.

My, oh my.

He felt a soft, subtle rise of pressure in his groin. Then the pressure was not so subtle, and he raised his hips toward whatever Angel-voice was doing down there.

With a shudder and a gasp he spilled over the edge, pumping fluids for what seemed a long, long time.

Then with a sigh he let himself relax back onto the bed.

"Feel better now, honey?" the angel voice asked.

"I damn sure do."

She chuckled again and moved up beside him. "Sure you do."

Longarm reached to put an arm around her. He touched her shoulder and slid his hand across her back. And on across it. And on a ways further without managing to come to the end of things so he could cuddle her.

His eyes popped open.

25

Angel-voice was peering happily into his eyes from a distance of only a few inches away.

She had a face like a moon. Except bigger. Not as seen from a distance, either. More like as seen if a guy was *standing* on it.

Angel-voice was the largest female Longarm had ever seen.

He amended that thought. She was the largest *human* he had ever seen.

He blinked and squinted.

Angel-voice chuckled. "Feeling better, honey?"

"Uh, yes, ma'am." It was the truth. He did feel better. Good enough, in fact, to get the hell out of here now.

She smiled and patted his cheek. Longarm felt himself blush.

He sat up. He could see now that Angel-voice was naked too. He wondered if he was going to be sick again.

That would be damn inconsiderate, though. He managed a smile somehow.

"You sure are one sweet man," Angel-voice said happily.

Longarm stifled an impulse to groan. What in *hell* had he done last night?

He smiled again and stood, a little shaky but almighty happy to be on his feet and off that bed. *What* had he done.

For that matter, what had *she* done this morning? He decided he probably didn't want to know anyway.

His clothes were draped with care over the back of a straight chair. Longarm hurried into them and felt much, much better when he was clothed. He wished Angel-voice would cover herself too, but it wouldn't do to ask. He smiled at her instead.

"Will I see you again, honey?" She sounded wistfully hopeful.

26

"Maybe," Longarm said with a smile. He settled the gun belt at his waist and shrugged into his coat.

He would have preferred to just walk out now, but he couldn't bring himself to do that. Angel-voice had been nice to him. And he'd probably been pretty disgusting at the time. No, he couldn't just turn his back and walk out on her now.

Instead he settled the Stetson on his head and went back to the bedside.

He bent over and gave her a brief kiss good-bye. Her eyes looked awfully bright. Damn, he hoped she wasn't crying. "Bye."

"Good-bye, honey."

He let himself out, hoping he would find himself in some part of Denver that he recognized so he could find his way home now without the embarrassment of having to ask someone where the hell he was this morning.

It wasn't until he was out on the sidewalk that he remembered he was unemployed.

Whatever else happened last night, he had sure managed to forget his miseries for a while.

He supposed that had to count for something.

He experimented with whistling as he walked down the street in search of recognizable territory, but that just brought the pounding back into his head, so he quit the tune abruptly.

What he needed, he decided, was coffee.

And then, inevitably, he supposed he was going to have to drag this whole mess out and look it over so he could decide what, if anything, to do about it.

It was just as well that he couldn't whistle right now. He no longer wanted to anyway.

Chapter 6

Longarm turned slightly to the side and propped the heels of his boots on the seat of a chair at the next table. There was nobody else in the place to mind. It was past 2 P.M. according to his Ingersol, and the café was empty except for one unemployed former deputy. He was just now feeling up to putting something in his stomach.

The waiter approached and took his order with a raised eyebrow. "You want toast? Dry toast? No butter or anything? Just toast?"

"That's right. Just toast. Dry. And coffee."

The waiter shrugged and went away.

The thought of anything greasy, or any kind of real food for that matter, was enough to make Longarm's stomach churn.

He'd been thinking it over all morning. He did not have to make any decisions right away. He had a few dollars laid by. Enough that he could take his time about finding another job if he was reasonably frugal in the meantime. No more repeats of last night, for instance. He had no idea how much he spent last night, or on what, but his pockets were empty when he got home this morning. He'd had to go by the bank just to get money enough that he could buy himself some toast and coffee now.

The best thing, of course, would be if Billy Vail cooled off and calmed down and decided Longarm should come back onto the payroll.

That was what Longarm truly hoped would happen.

If not, well, he could always find a job. He hadn't been a lawdog forever. He'd done other work before, and he could do other work again. Or for that matter he could poke around and see who might need somebody to carry a badge at a local level. A town marshal, say, or a county deputy somewhere. It wouldn't be the same. Not hardly. But he wasn't too proud to do it.

And anyway, Billy should come around when they got around to realizing that Longarm had been right about Big Little.

No matter what Billy and the damned political friends of Mack Bowen said, Long still didn't believe that poor old Big shot anybody.

Once they figured that out, Billy would be doing some apologizing, by damn.

That thought made Longarm feel better.

Billy *owed* him an apology.

Longarm damn sure figured to collect on that debt.

He grunted softly to himself and visualized United States Marshal William Vail making an abject apology with his head hung low and his hat in hand.

Yeah, that would just about square things.

The waiter delivered his coffee—the first sip tasted sour and oily—and said the toast would be out in a few minutes. Longarm thanked the man and reached for a *Rocky Mountain News* someone had left lying on the next table.

The first story he saw on the front page of the newspaper was about the post office robbery and Mack Bowen's murder, of course.

It was big news in Denver as well as in Englewood, what with the fact of the robbery itself, and then on top of that Bowen's close political connections with most of the bigwigs in this part of the state.

The newspaper reporter gave a colorful account of the robbery, making up in enthusiasm what he lacked in facts, and managed to give the impression that the un-named female postal patron—Mrs. Frake, that would be—was as good as raped at gunpoint by one of the holdup men. The reporter accomplished that feat without using one word that could be considered offensive or suggestive. Or libelous.

According to the news story, the gunmen had made off with over two thousand dollars in cash, a fistful of blank postal money orders and one first-class mail sack of unknown content.

The reporter identified the leader of the gang as one Chester William "Wig" Little, a farm laborer "of notorious reputation in the vicinity, according to informed sources."

Longarm grunted again at that one. Notorious, my ass, he thought. And they didn't even get his name right. Called him Wig instead of Big.

Still, the news story went on, a posse consisting of Englewood police, county and federal officers, was scheduled to depart on a manhunt for this "Wig" Little shortly after press time last night.

So by now, Longarm thought, poor old Big was sitting in a jail somewhere and probably didn't even understand why.

Mercifully, though, the newspaper story said nothing about the failure of one particular federal officer to arrest "Wig" when he had the chance, and nothing either about that said officer being fired as a result.

Of course, the only reason the reporter wouldn't have put that into the story was that he didn't know about it. Yet. Longarm grimaced. He wasn't particularly looking forward to being embarrassed in black and white. He might as well accept the idea that it was going to happen, though. In tomorrow's headlines, more than likely, right under where they would say that the murderous desperado "Wig" Little was arrested.

Longarm could live with that, though, as long as the story didn't have to say that "Wig" was shot while resisting arrest or something. Probably those possemen last night were riding on skittish emotions after learning that Bowen was dead. Mack had been popular in Englewood, mostly because he was part of the good-old-boy

30

crowd that handed out jobs when the political pork was being divvied out.

He thought about going over to the jail to see if Big was safely there or was in a pine box someplace by now. But he didn't want any of the boys at the jail gossiping behind his back now that he was on the outs. The hell with them. He could read about it in the *News* tomorrow, better yet in the *Post* when the afternoon editions hit the street. He would go see if he could buy one soon as he got done with his skimpy meal here. Maybe it was late enough by now that the *Post* would be out. If not, it wouldn't be long.

It surely did seem strange, though, to be at loose ends like this.

Longarm didn't like the feeling.

You would think a fellow would be feeling free and easy when there was nothing that he had to do. Like it was an unexpected vacation or something.

He wished he did feel that way about it.

The waiter finally got around to delivering his toast to the table. The stuff tasted like shit, but at least he was able to put it down without throwing it right back up again.

Yeah, this sure was the free and easy life, all right.

Longarm made a face and forced down another bite of the dry, half-burnt bread.

Chapter 7

"Killer at large. Killer at large. Getcher paper here. Killer at large."

"Boy. Over here." Longarm took the freshly issued *Post* and gave the youngster a nickel. He carried the newspaper down the street without bothering to wait for his change, already poring over the front page.

The headline gave little more information than the news hawker had. For that matter, the story beneath the headline didn't add all that much either.

According to the *Post*, Chester "Big" Little, the man who shot Englewood postmaster Mack Bowen to death in a daylight robbery of the United States Post Office in that city, remained at large as of press time after escaping a force of officers who surrounded the Circle Y ranch late last night . . . and blah, blah, blah.

The rest of the rather lengthy story was basically a rehash of what the *News* already had in their morning edition, the main difference being that the afternoon newspaper had at least gotten Big's nickname correct.

Now how in hell did Big get away? Longarm wondered.

And why?

A chill of sudden concern shot through him.

Big wasn't likely to have slipped away after the posse arrived at the ranch last night. The newspaper surely would have said something dramatic about shots being fired and all that if Big had been there when the arresting officers had arrived.

That meant Big probably ran before they came looking.

And *that* meant that Big Little must be a damn sight smarter than Longarm ever gave him credit for being.

Smart enough—sly enough, anyway—to smile and nod and pull a whole fleeceful of wool right smack over Longarm's eyes yesterday afternoon.

Big must have shot Bowen after all.

And then-Deputy Custis Long had let him get away with it.

Longarm scowled, his expression dark enough to make a woman on the sidewalk avert her eyes and suddenly change direction.

He rolled the newspaper into a thin prod and slapped his palm with it several times. Then, with an audible grunt, he spun around and started back the way he had just come.

It occurred to him that the horse he had rented in Englewood yesterday was still here in Denver. He had to return the animal to the livery anyway. And if he was going that far, well, he might as well ride a few miles further.

The idea that he might really have fucked up was not a pleasant one to contemplate. And with or without Billy Vail's authority he intended to take another look at Big Little and the charges against the man.

Longarm touched the brim of his hat respectfully. "Ma'am."

"Marshal Long, isn't it?" Mrs. Vieren asked.

"Yes, ma'am." It didn't seem worthwhile going into long explanations at the moment.

"You'll be wanting to see Patrick, I suppose."

"Yes, ma'am, if it's convenient."

"He's out in the barns somewhere, Marshal. Just call out if you can't find him."

"Thank you, ma'am." Longarm touched the brim of his Stetson again and backed away. Mrs. Vieren went back inside the house.

Her husband was nowhere to be found along the row

of stud barns. Longarm finally found him out at the mare end of the setup, cleaning out the stall where Big had kept his "awful purty" filly. The stall was empty now, and Pat was sweeping the floor. A loaded manure spreader held the bedding that Longarm had walked on yesterday, but no fresh bedding material was being laid down.

"H'lo, Longarm." Pat leaned his broom against a side wall. "I expect I can guess what you're here for. Same as everybody else, right?"

Longarm nodded. "I guess I am, Pat."

"Well, I don't know what to tell you any more than I already told them. Big was here when Althea and I left yesterday morning. I'd already sent Tom off with the Clydesdale for a late breeding. It was a mare he covered earlier. Damn sow slipped her foal though she'd taken before. The owner wanted her bred again this late so he wouldn't lose a whole year on the mare.

"Anyway, Tom hooked the Clyde to the cart and went off. While Althea was getting her lists together I came out and told Big to give the Clyde's stall a good cleaning while it was empty. He said he would, and for that matter the stall was good and clean when I got around to looking at it this morning."

"The Clyde would be Tartan Hi Boy."

"Damn. I'm surprised you'd remember that, Longarm."

"Truth is, I didn't. I came out to talk to Big yesterday afternoon. He was working in the stall then."

"You talked to Big? After the . . . after Mr. Bowen was killed?"

"Yes, I did," Longarm admitted.

"But . . ."

"I knew Mack had been shot, Pat. I knew Big was suspected of it. I won't try to tell you otherwise. I came out here, and I talked with Big, and I decided he hadn't done it. I'm sorry to say that I rode away then. I didn't try to place him under arrest."

34

Pat Vieren did not give Longarm the stark, staring disapproval that Longarm fully expected. If anything, the Circle Y owner looked sympathetic. "I'd have done the same thing myself, Longarm. I surely would have."

"I just...I don't know how I could have been so badly fooled."

"If you were. Frankly, Longarm, I don't believe Big shot anybody. Not Mr. Bowen and not anybody else. I just don't think the man had it in him to be hurtful."

"I wish I could believe you were right, Pat, but...the way he took off running and everything. It doesn't look good. A man doesn't run from the law without reason. Besides, how would he have known the law was after him? Or did you tell him when you got home last night?"

"I never saw Big again after yesterday morning," Vieren said, quashing that possible answer. "It was late when we got home. We went to Denver, did some shopping and stayed for supper at the Brown Palace. It's one of Althea's favorites, you see. So it was, oh, nine-thirty or so before we got back. I carried our packages inside and walked down to the bunkhouse to make sure everything was all right. That old bitch of a mare of Jack Heath's is a kicker, and I wanted to make sure Hi Boy hadn't got hurt when he was covering her.

"Tom was alone in the bunkhouse when I got there. He said he hadn't seen Big. That Big had left already when he got back, but that it was about dark by then, so he didn't think anything of it."

Vieren frowned. "Now wait a minute. I think I'm getting ahead of myself there. I guess at that time neither Tom nor me thought anything peculiar that Big was gone. I mean, there wasn't anybody at the house to cook dinner, and we're close enough to town that the hands can go in of an evening pretty much whenever they please. Both of them do, time to time.

"Big is, well, a little soft in the head, of course. But

35

he's a man grown, and he enjoys himself as much as anybody else. More, in a way, I think."

Longarm nodded. He knew what Pat meant. He had been in a saloon with Big once or twice in the past, and the big man was happy and cheerful, never holding back on his pleasures, whatever they might be.

"So I really didn't think anything about it that Tom said he hadn't seen Big. Nothing unusual about Big finishing his work for the day and riding into town after, particularly if he'd have to do his own cooking. He isn't much more for cooking than I am. So anyhow, Tom told me how the breeding went. Hi Boy covered the mare and didn't get himself kicked. Won't know for a while, of course, if the stupid cow took again or not.

"I got Tom's report and went back up to the house to help Althea put things away in the pantry. We were still busy doing that when the posse got here. They had the place surrounded before either of us knew there was anybody but us and Tom on the grounds. They came in quiet and ready, guns cocked and everything." He frowned. "Scared hell out of both of us, I'll tell you. We heard some shouting out in the yard . . . that's because they couldn't find Big in the bunkhouse and started yelling orders about searching all the buildings . . . and we went out and saw all these people running around with rifles and shotguns waving. We didn't know what to think. Luckily I recognized a couple of the deputies and called them over.

"They explained what was up. And why. Althea and me both could hardly believe it. And still can't. But of course we didn't know anything and wouldn't have tried to hide anything from them if we did. We told them the honest truth, just as I'm telling you now, Longarm. All we knew for sure or do yet is that Big isn't here right now."

"You don't think there's a chance that he would come back, do you, Pat?"

"Truthfully? No, I expect I don't, Longarm. I might

think otherwise, except as you can see for yourself this stall is empty. Big had a weanling filly in here that I gave him. Doted on the little crooked-foot thing, he did. When he left yesterday, he took the filly with him."

Longarm's interest quickened. "He took her with him?"

"Ayuh. I didn't know that till this morning when I came out to feed her. I thought I'd have to since Big wasn't here to do it himself. But she wasn't here. The door was closed and latched tight, but the stall was empty."

"That means he's cleared out, then. And that he can't figure to go very far. I saw that filly yesterday. She moves all right for having a leg like she does, but he wouldn't want to walk her very far on it. And besides, she's too little anyway to do much traveling. Come to think of it, how did Big go? Did he own any grown horses he could ride away?"

"Didn't own anything, exactly. He always used one of mine. Usually one of the big geldings I use to pull the spreader."

"Did he take one of them yesterday?"

"Hell, Longarm, I haven't looked."

Vieren led the way around to a corral on the south side of the property. There were several horses in it including three heavy bodied cob geldings and a pair of pensioned-off old stallions with drooping backs and graying muzzles.

"Agamemnon is gone," Vieren said.

"Pardon?"

"One of my geldings. Big, slow old thing that I use sometimes on the hay stacker when I need a little more oomph on the pusher. He's an old horse. I don't use him much anymore, but I keep him around. Nobody else would have any use for him either, and I don't like to put them down long as they can still chew. Comes to that, I just plain don't like to have to put a horse down.

I'll mostly keep them around till they die. I don't want to have to help them along. Big didn't either."

"Would this gelding be one Big would normally use to ride to town?"

Vieren shook his head quickly. "No, Aggie's too old and slow for a quick ride to town and back. Normally Big or Tom either one, would take that brown you see there or the big bay with the scar on his hip. That one. Not Agamemnon."

Longarm fingered his chin. "It looks like you had a horse stolen from you, Pat."

Vieren snorted. "The hell you say. Big has troubles enough without me adding to them. I'm not gonna call the law on him for horse theft too. Far as I'm concerned, he's welcome to Agamemnon as fair swap for the wages I owe him since payday. Fact of the matter is, it's a blessing for the old horse to feel useful again. They get to pining for work to do after they're retired, I swear they do. Big taking that horse is more a favor than anything else. You can tell them in Denver that I said so."

Longarm grinned. "You're a pretty good friend to have, Pat."

"Be different if I believed Big shot that man. Maybe. But I don't. I expect I'll have to hear him tell me with his own mouth that he shot Mack Bowen before I believe it. Regardless of what you or anybody else wants to say."

"My doubts are only from Big's actions since I left him yesterday, Pat. I want you to understand that, and I hope you won't hold against me whatever I might have to do. One thing I can promise you sure: If I bring Big in, it won't be laid over the back of a horse or hauled in a box if there's any way I can avoid it."

"Ah, I know that, Longarm. I just . . . I just still don't believe that sweet, soft-headed man ever hurt anybody. That's all."

Longarm smiled. "I appreciate what you're saying,

Pat. Look, would it bother you if I took a look in the bunkhouse now? I'd like to see the things Big left behind if the posse last night didn't carry it all off."

"Didn't carry anything off," Vieren said. "Sure, we'll go look. Maybe it'll help settle my mind on the subject too."

The Circle Y owner led the way back through the buildings toward the bunkhouse Big Little and Tom Lee had shared, until yesterday.

Chapter 8

Longarm was grim when he marched into the United States Marshal's office in the Federal Building. He looked like a man on his way to a date with the executioner.

"Longarm!" Henry looked up in surprise, then averted his eyes and looked down toward his desk again.

It was late, hours past quitting time in virtually all the other offices in the building, but Henry was still at his desk.

"I need to see Marshal Vail," Longarm said formally, unwilling to call Billy by a nickname now. "His lights are on. I take it he's still working?"

Henry nodded. He looked uncomfortable.

"May I see him, please?"

"I'll, uh . . . ask."

For years Longarm's habit had been to barge into Billy's private office whether it was convenient or not. But that had been when Custis Long was Billy Vail's top deputy.

Henry left his desk, tapped lightly on Billy's door and slipped inside, closing it behind him. He came back out a moment later. "The marshal will see you," he said.

"Thank you."

Longarm knocked on the door frame and waited for an answer before he went inside.

"If you want your final pay, Long, it is being processed now. Probably by—"

"I came to give you an apology," Longarm said.

"What?"

"I came to apologize. I let you down. I used my own discretion where I shouldn't have. And I apologize for that." He stepped forward, pulled a revolver out of his waistband and laid it onto the polished surface of Billy's desk, careful lest the pitted, shiny steel of the old gun mar the surface of the wood.

"What's this?"

"It's a cap-and-ball Colts Navy revolver that's been converted to .38 rimfire cartridges."

"I can see that, but . . ."

"The gun was found hidden under the mattress of the bunk Chester Little slept in at the Circle Y ranch before he took off running last night."

"Oh," Billy said weakly.

"Joe Doyle and his people didn't think to search the bunkhouse last night. I expect they were in a hurry to get after Little. So they didn't find the gun."

"And you did? Today?"

Longarm nodded stiffly. "I did. And before you ask, I went out there today with the idea of proving to everybody, and to myself too, I suppose, that I was right to not put Little in irons. Instead, I found this. I brought it here because I knew you'd want to know about this evidence and . . . and because I owe you an apology for making too much of myself the other day. There's the evidence. I hope you'll accept the apology too."

Vail frowned. Then he sighed. "You know I will, Custis."

"Thank you." Longarm turned to go.

"Custis."

"Yes?"

"What are your plans?"

Longarm shrugged. "First thing, I expect to see if I can't find Chester Little. After that, well . . . I'll just have to see what happens then."

"You're going after him?"

"I'm the dumb son of a bitch who left him loose, aren't I? Of course I'm going after him."

"Wait a minute." Billy opened the top drawer of his desk and fished inside it. He pulled out a badge that Longarm certainly had reason to recognize and tossed it onto the desk between them. It hit beside the unblued steel and scarred wood of the Navy Colt and spun slowly for a moment before coming to rest.

"Are you sure you want to—"

"Damnit, Longarm, don't get me pissed again. Just take the badge and use it. I'll call the papers back on our . . . difficulty. So to speak."

"Yes, sir."

"And tell Doyle about this gun you found. I saw him earlier today, and he was about as long-faced as you over this Little. He needs to know about the gun too."

Longarm nodded and let himself out of Billy's private office.

Henry was sitting behind his own cluttered desk, but this time he looked Longarm in the eyes. He was grinning from ear to ear.

"Damnit, Henry, I always suspected you of eavesdropping."

"Welcome home, Longarm."

"Thanks, Henry."

Longarm's step was considerably lighter leaving the Federal Building than it had been arriving.

Chapter 9

It was late, but Longarm was much more eager than tired. He felt revitalized now and anxious to get on with things.

Big had to be somewhere in the Denver/Englewood vicinity. He wouldn't have taken off on a broken-down old horse and with a half-lame filly at his side if he intended to go very far. So he had to be somewhere nearby. The task was to find him.

There were several possibilities. In the past Longarm had run into Big Little now and again in the run-down saloons near the Denver stockyards and also in some of the cowboy joints on the south side of Englewood.

Either area offered a logical place to begin looking for Big. Since he had to talk to Joe Doyle about the Navy Colt anyway, Longarm headed first for Englewood. He was unsure of the late train schedules and still had the rented horse, so he ignored the quicker and easier transportation offered by the rails and bumped the gelding into a road jog that ate up the distance between the neighboring towns in less than two hours.

Even so it was nearly midnight before Longarm rode into Englewood and was finally able to return the horse to the livery.

"You wouldn't know where I can find Sergeant Joe Doyle, would you?"

"Now?" The hostler was sleepy-eyed and none too happy about being wakened to tend to another animal.

"Yes, now."

"Hell, mister, I dunno. Try the p'lice station. They could tell you."

Longarm thanked him and walked down that way. He had rented the horse on a government voucher, so that was already taken care of.

There was a night lamp burning inside the Englewood police station, but there was no one at the desk. Longarm let himself in and paused to listen. Yellow light and the sound of low voices came through a doorway toward the back of the station. Apparently the officers on night duty were congregated back there. Longarm followed the sounds.

"Good evening, gentlemen."

One of them jumped with surprise and dropped his cards. He had three nines in the hand he showed. There were three of them at the table playing poker, a sergeant and two patrolmen. The sergeant looked distinctly uncomfortable to be found playing cards when he was on duty.

"Something we can do for you, mister?"

"I'm looking for Joe Doyle."

"Joe's out with the posse," the sergeant said.

Longarm raised an eyebrow and waited for the man to go on.

"Him and some other boys are trying to track that Little fella that murdered our postmaster the other day," the sergeant explained. "Cut his tracks this morning, they did, an' said they'd follow the son of a bitch to the ends of the earth."

"Or hard ground, whichever come first," one of the patrolmen mumbled under his breath. Longarm got the impression the patrolman didn't think much of the tracking abilities of the possemen. Perhaps, though, he had his reasons.

"I'll check back in the morning, then. Thanks." Longarm left the three of them to their game, wondering as he left the place if the men in that room were the entire force on duty in Englewood at the moment. The town would be burglar heaven if all the night cops spent

44

their working hours playing poker when they should have been out patroling the streets. Not his problem, thank goodness.

He stopped on the sidewalk outside the police station and lighted a cheroot, taking his time about it and mulling over the possibilities.

Doyle and his posse were larruping who knew where in pursuit of a man who almost certainly had to be somewhere fairly close to where Longarm was standing right at this moment. Longarm consulted his Ingersol—it was 12:17 A.M.—and turned south toward the honky-tonk district. Englewood's cops might not care, but that end of town would still be lively. There was always the chance that someone there might know Big's habits well enough to put Longarm on the scent.

"Rye whiskey."

"Half a bit," the barman said. He waited to see Longarm's money before he poured.

"You know a guy named Big Little?" Longarm asked before the bartender could turn away.

"Mister, everybody around here knows Big." The man did not sound particularly friendly about it.

"I need to get a message to him."

"Fuck you," the barman said without emphasis.

"You're a friend of his, then?"

The bartender turned away. Longarm took hold of his elbow, not roughly but with firm insistence. "I'm not quite through, neighbor."

"You're through," somebody to the side assured him.

There were three or four cowboys pressing closer now. They had been quietly drinking further down the bar. Now they were interested in the conversation.

"We don't need your kind around here right now," a second cowboy said.

"And what kind is that?" Longarm asked.

"Bounty hunters ain't welcome here, mister. Ol' Big

45

might or might not've done what they say. That ain't up to us to work out. Point is, Big was a friend of ours, of all of us here, an' we don't wanta see the guy put down before he can say his piece."

"Bounty? What bounty?"

One of the cowboys looked like he wanted to spit. "Don't try and tell us that—"

"If it makes a difference, neighbor, Big is a friend of mine too," Longarm told them. He pulled out his badge and flashed it. "I'd like to see him brought back in one piece just as much as you would. Now what's this about a bounty?"

The cowboys seemed to relax at least a little once they knew the tall man in front of them was not a bounty hunter looking for Big's scalp.

"A bunch of the bigshot politicians have put up a two-thousand-dollar reward on Big, mister. Dead or alive. And they say Mr. Bowen's family is gonna add to that."

"Shit," Longarm blurted. Quick notoriety and the promise of easy reward money never failed to bring a flock of amateurs into a hunt. Most of them, in Longarm's experience, were possessed of more ammunition than brains. One of that stripe was apt to think more in terms of bullets than handcuffs.

"There's been a bunch of bounty hunters in here already tonight, Marshal," one of the cowboys explained.

"We got nothing against the law," another said, "but we don't wanta see Big gunned down by one o' them sons o' bitches. If he done what they say, and I got my doubts about that, then I suppose he's gotta be brought in for trial. But I don't wanta see the guy dead before he gets here."

"I agree," Longarm said. "That's why I'm here."

"They say there's a posse already chasing him."

"Hell, Tommy, those boys couldn't find a horse turd in a sugar bowl. Bunch o' damn city fellers."

"I don't know that I'd trust them t' bring Big in alive neither," another put in. "They're all het up an' excited an' mostly scared. They're as likely t' shoot as some o' them bounty bastards."

"It probably would be a good idea if I could get to Big first," Longarm put in. "I don't believe Big would try to shoot if he saw it was me, no matter how scared he is. We know each other pretty well."

"What'd you say your name was, Marshal?"

Longarm hadn't said but he did now.

"Hell, you're the guy that talked to Big after the holdup an' let him go, ain't you?"

"How did you know that?"

"Ain't you seen the *News* this evening?"

"The *News* is a morning paper."

"Yeah, but they put out an extra. Say, I thought you got fired off your job for lettin' Big go."

"You can't believe everything you read, can you." He didn't feel like going into all the details with these boys right at the moment.

"I guess maybe you ain't a gunner, mister. You'd really bring Big in alive?"

"Absolutely."

The cowboys passed glances back and forth. Finally one of them nodded. "How can we help you, Marshal?"

"Bartender, bring us that bottle of rye and some glasses." Longarm led the cowboys to a table and sat down with them.

"What I'd like you boys to do," he told them, "is to tell me everything you know about Big. What he likes. Where he goes. Who his friends are. Everything you can think of."

"You really think that will help, Marshal?"

"Right now," Longarm said truthfully, "I think it is the best chance Big Little has to stay alive long enough to face his accusers. Especially if there's a reward out on him and the bounty hunters are getting interested."

47

With little hesitation, and that quickly dispelled once they warmed to the subject, the cowboys began reminiscing about their friend Big and all his quirks and habits. They talked through that first bottle of rye whiskey and most of the way through a second before they were done.

Chapter 10

Longarm leaned back and tilted the last of the whiskey into his glass. It was past two in the morning, and the cowboys had just left.

The lean young men — most cowboys were young, they almost had to be to stand the rigors of their trade — would ride half an hour to as much as two hours to get home to their bunks, then crawl out at five o'clock or so to have breakfast finished and a horse saddled by dawn, ready for their day's work.

Longarm did not envy them the way they would feel tomorrow. He had done the same himself when he was their age, and at the time hadn't thought a thing about it. Now he was fairly sure the routine life of a cowhand would kill him.

He sipped at the whiskey. It hadn't been a particularly good grade of rye when he first tasted it, but it had begun to grow on him over the past hour or so. While he drank he mulled over what the boys had told him.

Mostly they had told stories of Big and of themselves. More happy memories than real information. The few things they said that might be helpful were like flakes of free gold captured in a pan of black mud: damned rare.

Part of the problem was that Big Little was no deep thinker and certainly not a serious conversationalist. He wasn't secretive. He just didn't have all that much to say about himself. Big preferred to talk about horses and horse shoeing and horse doctoring and horse breeding and horse training.

From what the local cowboys had picked up over the

past year or two that Big had been around Englewood and Denver, Big came originally from either southern Missouri or northern Arkansas. Everyone was a little unclear about which it was. Possibly he had lived both places as a boy.

From there he must have drifted down to Texas to learn how to cowboy because he had mentioned people and brands from the saltgrass Gulf area and from the thorny brush country of south Texas.

All the boys remembered hearing Big say on more than one occasion that he was working cattle in the Bosque Redondo country in New Mexico when he got caught in a stampede. His horse was knocked down and trampled. That was when Big's leg was permanently crippled and why he walked with a limp now.

"Never heard ol' Big moan about his leg, that was just one o' the breaks o' the game," one of the boys said, "but he sure useta feel bad that he'd let his horse get tore up by them cows. Broke the critter's canon an' got its one eye trampled out so it had to be put down. Big still feels bad 'bout that. It's why he's got no use for cows anymore. He onliest likes t' work with horses an' has ever since that time, but it ain't on account of his own leg but that the horse had t' be put down. He sure did feel bad 'bout that."

Apparently he came up to Colorado through the Trinidad area. They had heard him talk about working as a wrangler down along the Picketwire. Then he'd been an assistant groom—whatever the hell one of those was—for General Palmer. Then on north until he lit here in the Denver and Englewood neighborhood. He had hooked on with Pat Vieren at the Circle Y by the time any of them got acquainted with him. Just the same as Longarm had, the cowboys he knew in the area liked him just as soon as they met him. Big was easy to like.

No, none of them had ever seen him get into a fight. No one had ever seen him hurt anyone or anything or ever say that he wanted to.

"Most guys see a guy Big's size, they kinda walk wide around him if they're feeling proddy," one of the boys said. "O' course there's always the kind o' asshole that thinks a guy that big just has t' be tried." He chuckled. "I seen an ol' boy like that try an' take Big on one night just, oh, a month, month an' a half ago maybe. It was down the street at the Aces Up.

"This ol' boy was likkered up pretty good, I think. An' he gets to eyeballin' Big an' walkin' around him in circles an' sayin' how he can whip anybody in the damn place an' he'll prove it by whipping up on the biggest guy in the place, which o' course was Big. I mean, any place Big walked into, he was just naturally the biggest guy there. Which otherwise I s'pose this drunk woulda been but not with Big there. Y'know?"

Longarm's new friends were fairly well liquored up themselves by then. They all looked at their friend and nodded solemnly.

"So this ol' boy, he keeps sayin' how he's gonna whip Big. An' Big, he just grins an' ignores the guy. The guy wants to push it, so he up and tells Big to stand an' take his whuppin', an' then he throws a punch. Squared off an' braced himself an' got himself all set an' throws a real beauty of a right hand into Big's gut, which is the soft spot on most big guys.

"Ol' Big, he stands there an' chuckles an' grins, an' the guy's fist hits so hard it hurts him—the guy, I mean, not Big—an' he squalls an' hollers an' hops around holdin' his hand 'cause he's hurt himself. Big looks sorry 'bout havin' hurt the feller, but he sure ain't mad. Which makes this drunken feller all the madder. So he says he's gonna get that big sumbitch one way or th' other, an' he hauls out his belly gun. He's got this rusty ol' fishin' sinker of a pistol, but it looks like it can shoot, an' it ain't the pretty part that hurts you.

"Well us in the bar there, we start t' get excited too. But Big don't. He sees the guy fetch iron so he reaches out an' takes the gun away from this guy an' grins an' turns the thing sideways. He takes a good holt on it an' twists, an' he snaps the hammer off sideways. Just busted it right off. Then he hands the busted gun back t' the guy an' asks if his hand is feelin' better now.

"You shoulda heard the howl that went up in that place, lemme tell you. This drunk . . . he was a big guy himself, mind . . . he gets all red in the face an' hauls his ass outa there but *quick*. Haven't seen him around since, neither."

The cowboys got a kick out of that one. The story touched off another memory, and they were off and running again.

Longarm heard them all out and told them good-bye and sat pondering the little he had learned. He hadn't gleaned much from the two hours of talk. But at least it gave him a little more knowledge about the big, easy-going man who had become his quarry. Maybe that would be worth something.

By the time he finished his drink the last customers were drifting toward the doors, and the barman was working alone behind the counter cleaning up.

Longarm gave the guy a hand by carrying his own empty glasses and bottles over and setting them on the bar. He started to turn away, but the bartender stopped him. "Marshal?"

"Yes?"

The bartender looked around the place to make sure the last customers were gone. Apparently he did not want anyone to think that he might tell stories on his patrons. Even if he would

"You really figure to bring Big in safe?"

"I do."

"Talk to Sally Anne."

"Pardon me?"

"Sally Anne Hufnagel. She's Big's ladyfriend. She might be able to help."

"Where could I find Sally Anne Hufnagel?"

"She's a washerwoman. She's no hoor, if that's what

52

you're wondering. Independent minded, maybe, but no hoor. I happen to know Big's been sneaking over there of an evening pretty regular lately. So you might ask her."

"I will, thanks. Where can I find her?"

The bartender gave Longarm directions to the Hufnagel shack and then went quickly back to his cleaning chores as if he were ashamed of volunteering to be helpful.

Longarm checked his watch on his way out. It was much too late to be calling on a woman who was "no hoor," particularly if she took in laundry to earn her living and would have to be up and working at an early hour.

Rather than trying to get back to Denver for what little remained of the night and then return to Englewood at first light, he decided to get a room and be on hand to talk with Miss Hufnagel first thing.

He yawned and turned toward the nearest hotel instead of the railroad depot.

Chapter 11

"Ma'am." Longarm touched the brim of his Stetson.

"Yes?" Her expression and her tone of voice were deeply suspicious. It was early, not yet seven o'clock, but already her face was flushed and damp from exertion and from the influence of tubs of boiling water. The underarms of her plain dress were stained dark in a most unladylike manner, and a strand of hair escaped from her bun and lay wet and limp against the side of her neck.

Otherwise, he realized, she might have been considered attractive if somewhat on the scrawny side. She had walnut-brown hair with hints and glints of red in it and large, bright hazel eyes. Her features were finely drawn, almost patrician.

"Mrs. Hufnagel?" he inquired politely.

"Miss Hufnagel," she corrected. "And yes. I am she."

I am she. It wasn't exactly every washerwoman who would put it that way.

Behind her he could see and smell the steam from her tubs, and the odor that reached him through the doorway of the run-down house was heavy with the biting scent of lye soap and wood smoke. The yard beside the house was a maze of ropes and wooden clothesline props, still empty at this early hour.

"Well?" she asked crisply. "You haven't brought any laundry. Or do you expect me to pick it up, too? I haven't time for that. If you want me to wash for you, you can at least bring your things here."

"My name is Long, miss. Custis Long. It isn't

54

laundry I've come about, but Big Little. I was hoping you might know where I could find him."

Sally Anne Hufnagel sniffed and drew herself up to her full height, which he realized was not very great. She somehow seemed taller than she was, although she came only chest high on him. "Another bounty hunter, I presume." She made it sound like she was saying something dirty.

"No, ma'am," he said quickly. She was already reaching for the door and seemed quite fully prepared to slam it in his face. "I'm a deputy U.S. marshal, miss. And I don't want to do Big any harm. I just want to talk to him."

"With that?" She pointed toward the Colt that rode dark and deadly in the cross-draw rig at Longarm's waist.

"No, ma'am," he said again. "Look, could I please talk to you?"

"I have nothing to say to you or to anyone else who wants to harm that poor man."

"Miss Hufnagel, I want to *help* Big, not harm him."

She sniffed again in disbelief.

"Please. Just let me talk to you. You won't have to tell me anything that you don't want. Just let me talk with you for a few minutes." He tried to charm her with a smile, but he got the impression that Miss Sally Anne Hufnagel was not easily charmed.

She sniffed again. But she did step back from the door and motion for him to follow. "I'll not interrupt my work for you," she said coldly, "but I shall listen." She went to the nearest of several steaming tubs and used a long wooden prod to stir whatever was bubbling in there.

Longarm trailed uncomfortably behind and began to speak to Miss Hufnagel's stiff back.

"Thank you." She took another sweet bun, acting half ashamed of her own hunger, and wolfed it. Longarm

55

had gone out to buy an assortment of pastries and a quantity of already roasted and ground coffee after Miss Hufnagel refused to take time away from her work to have a restaurant meal with him. After seeing how hungry the woman was he wished he had bought more.

"Truly I apologize for the way I acted earlier," she said, as she already had several times before. "You just don't know the things people are saying about Chester."

"Yes, ma'am."

"That poor man couldn't possibly have harmed anyone," she insisted. That too was a much repeated statement. "I am so frightened for him now, though, what with the bounty posted. It is cruel, Mr. Long. It is absolutely cruel of them to be hunting Chester like a poor innocent deer or..."

"Yes, ma'am." He gathered that Miss Hufnagel didn't hold with hunting of any sort, whether for man or meat. She considered all of it cruel.

"The thing is," he repeated—it was the argument he had used to win her cooperation—"I want to bring him in so he can tell his side of it, but I want to make sure he's alive so he *can* tell his tale. It's no good if Big is gunned down by some idiot with the bounty on his mind."

"I understand that." She sighed. "Probably I should know better than to believe you, Mr. Long. Lord knows, I've been disappointed often enough before when I accepted a man's word for anything." She did not choose to elaborate. "But I shall take you at face value and help you if I can."

"It's for Big's own good."

"If I did not believe that, sir, I most surely would show you the door."

"Yes, ma'am."

She reached for another sweet bun and dunked an edge of it in the strong coffee she had brewed. "As I already told you, I have not seen Chester since the... incident in town. Nor have I heard from him. I would expect to, Mr. Long. Chester has become a dear friend this past month or so since we met. A dear friend. Although despite whatever you may have heard that brought you to my door this morning, there is no physical relationship between us." She said it matter-of-factly. "I met Chester when he asked me to do his washing. He is such a sweet and thoughtful man. He helped me with some lifting and carrying simply because he saw it was difficult for me. And we talked a little. About horses, which are his primary interest. I mentioned something I had read on the subject and suggested he read the article himself. I told him where he could find it. He confessed that he could not read and expressed a lifelong desire to learn, and I offered to teach him. He has been coming frequently since then and applying himself diligently if without quick success. Can you believe that? A grown man who cannot read?"

She sounded quite offended by the idea, although in point of fact there were a great many fully grown adults of Longarm's acquaintance, both men and women, who could not read their own names. The notion did not shock him nearly so much as it seemed to disturb Sally Anne Hufnagel.

"I have come to know Chester well, I believe," she said. "I can tell you categorically that he did not commit murder or any other crime."

"Yes, ma'am." He wasn't going to argue the point with her. Although all the available evidence including that Longarm discovered himself said that Big Little did indeed commit murder and sundry other crimes.

"I can also tell you that if Chester were in hiding anywhere in this vicinity he would surely come to me. He has not done so. He must surely be elsewhere, Mr. Long."

"Yes, ma'am."

"If he does come to me or communicate with me somehow, I shall surely advise him to meet with you.

57

You can ask him yourself about his alleged involvement in these crimes. If you know Chester, then you know also that he would not lie to you. I do not believe he would know how to lie."

"Yes, ma'am." Longarm left the buns alone—whatever was left over would be a welcome addition to Miss Hufnagel's pantry—but helped himself to more coffee. That, he reasoned, would only turn bitter if left in the pot for later.

"I would like him to sit down and talk with you," she said. "And as quickly as possible. If any of those horrid bounty men find him before you do . . ." She shuddered.

Longarm's best guess was that Sally Anne Hufnagel was telling him the complete truth when she said she had not seen Big and did not know where he was. Damnit. He'd been hoping she might be able to help him. But then, maybe she still could. If only she was right and Big might yet get in touch with her.

He told her where she could reach him. "Naturally I'll reimburse you for your expense and trouble if you have to send a wire," he added.

"That is not necessary," she informed him primly. "I shall do whatever I can to aid Chester."

"Yes, ma'am." He thanked her for her trouble and left.

Oddly, though, there was something about Sally Anne Hufnagel that kept her in his thoughts as he walked back toward the center of town. She was not all that pretty, exactly. There was something about her, though, that was intriguing. She seemed unique, a woman entirely her own.

One thing about her that was entirely common, though, was her loyalty to Big. Like the big, slow-witted man's other friends, she seemed thoroughly convinced of his innocence. Longarm no longer had that luxury of opinion.

But he had to admit that his doubts were growing once again.

He wondered if Billy Vail or perhaps the local officers had any new information that would help shed more light on the case. He altered his direction toward the police station, deciding to stop there before he returned to Denver. Just in case there was something new.

Chapter 12

There was damn sure something new going on when Longarm got to the Englewood police station.

He was no more than inside the door before the sergeant behind the desk said, "You're Long?"

"That's right."

"There's been messages asking for you over half o' Colorado this morning, Deputy. That son of a bitch Little's done it again."

"What?"

"In Aurora this time. First thing when the post office was opening. Little and his gang hit just as the doors was opened. Word come on the telegraph better'n an hour ago, and Denver's been looking for you practic'ly just as quick an' several times since. They want you t' haul your ass to Aurora. But *quick*."

Longarm was frowning as he did a quick about-face and hauled his ass for the railroad depot and Aurora.

Much of the confusion had ebbed by the time Longarm arrived on the scene. The usual crowd of citizens that gathered at the site of any disaster had disbursed. The post office was closed for the remainder of the day. Longarm's badge gained his admission.

Billy Vail was there. So was Smiley. So were several local officers. They were all talking to a distraught and shaken civilian. Behind the counter a man with a mop and bucket was busy trying to clean a red stain off the floor. So far he had managed to reduce scarlet to pink.

"Oh, shit," Longarm muttered. "What happened?"

Vail frowned. "Your boy Little did it again, Longarm. He and his gang hit as the front door was being unlocked. They played it just the way they did before. Little came in first with his gun out and a mask over his head. The door had been opened by the clerk. His name is Fred Samson. He saw the masks and the drawn gun and turned to run. He managed to get as far as the counter, and Little shot him in the back. The bullet passed through his lung. The doctors say he may or may not make it. We won't know about that for a while.

"The gang came in in a rush. One of them knocked Jesse down on the floor in a corner there."

Jesse, Longarm assumed, would be the civilian they were all talking with, probably the postmaster.

"The rest of them stripped the contents of the drawers. Money, stamps, everything there was. Little took the mailbag."

"Why was there a mailbag?" Longarm asked. "There wasn't anything going out first thing in the morning, was there?"

"Outgoing mail is stored in a bag in the safe overnight," the man named Jesse said. "We don't leave it unprotected, of course. Everything collected since the last bag out is kept in the safe until the next outgoing shipment."

"Was the safe open when they hit, or did they make you open it for them?"

"It was already open, of course. We have to open it each morning to take out our stamps and the cash drawer. We protect all of that overnight, of course."

"I've already asked all this shit," Smiley said glumly.

"Sure, but I haven't."

"Suit yourself." Smiley shrugged and turned away.

"This doesn't look good," Billy Vail said.

"I know, damnit. If I'd done what I should have to start with . . ."

"I'm trying to remember that that is all water under the bridge, Longarm. I can't say it will be easy to do if Samson dies, though."

61

Longarm felt thoroughly miserable. "How do you know it was Little, Billy?"

Vail frowned. "The description is certainly the same," the marshal said. "There aren't very many men that size, after all. And that distinctive hat."

"Did anybody see his face?"

"Little was masked. As before." Billy gave him a sharp look. No one, Billy Vail included, was much interested at the moment in hearing Custis Long question the identity of the postal robber who now had hit, and shot, twice in a span of days.

"What kind of gun was he using this time?" Longarm asked, shifting direction quickly.

He was mildly hoping, though, that once again a converted Navy Colt would have been used by the big gunman. Because Big Little's Navy was in Billy Vail's possession now and had been since yesterday.

The postmaster answered. "It was a big one," he said. "Dark. Almost black." That didn't fit the Navy described in the Englewood robbery. That one was supposed to have had the bluing mostly worn off. Like Big's did.

"Old?"

The postmaster shook his head. "It didn't look old to me. I don't know much about guns, though. I would say that it didn't look old. It was big. I certainly remember that."

Longarm grunted. "What about the getaway?"

"Same as before," Billy told him. "They had the horses outside. They hit fast and rode out even faster. There is a posse chasing them now. They rode east out of town. After that . . ." He shrugged. "We won't know anything until the posse gets back."

There was, of course, no point in going helling after them. By now the trail was hours old, and they would have to depend on the quickly assembled posse from Aurora to run the robbers down if they could.

"Shit," Longarm said.

"I agree," Billy Vail said dryly.

"I'm sorry, Billy. Damnit to hell I'm sorry."

Vail frowned.

"I'll find him, Billy. I swear, if he is anywhere in Colorado right now, I'll find him and bring him in."

Billy Vail did not bother to answer.

Longarm might be back on the payroll, but that did not necessarily mean he was back in Billy's good graces. Not now that a second robbery and shooting had occurred.

Longarm turned miserably away and went back out into the afternoon sunshine. There were times, he realized, when the company of strangers could be more comfortable than the presence of friends.

Chapter 13

He had to find Big before anymore damage was done. He *had* to.

Right. But how the hell do you go about finding someone when they had the whole northeast quarter of Colorado to hide in and didn't want to be found?

Denver and the maze of neighboring towns and communities alone had thousands of backyard barns and carriage sheds where a man could hide a broken-down old horse and a weanling filly. Literally thousands. A man could spend a lifetime trying to look into each one of them and never gain a thing except by blind luck. Longarm did not particularly believe in blind luck as a law enforcement tool.

The Aurora posse was trying the direct approach and chasing Big and his gang of post office robbers. With luck maybe they would accomplish something. But Longarm wasn't going to count on that form of luck either. The Englewood posse hadn't been able to catch the bunch. Likely the Aurora crowd wouldn't either.

Longarm frowned as he rode the train back to Denver. Damnit. Big had to be out there *some*where.

He left the short-haul local at the Denver station and took a cab to his rooming house. He wanted a bath and a change of clothes and needed time to do some thinking.

When he left his room he was carrying his saddlebags and McClellan saddle with him. He wanted to be as mobile as necessary from now on, and the hell with inconvenience.

• • •

"Ma'am." He touched the brim of his hat and smiled.

"Mr. Long. Please come in." Sally Anne Hufnagel stepped back from the doorway and motioned him inside.

"I took the liberty of bringing some supper with me. Hope you don't mind, but I've been on the go all day and haven't had much time to eat." His smile made it believable although it was not strictly true. "There's enough for two if you'd care to join me."

He had stopped at a local café and got them to pack a basket dinner of roast beef and fresh rolls and mashed potatoes that were probably getting cold by now. He'd had them pack enough for four, actually.

She seemed pleased. She quickly cleared stacks of freshly ironed shirts off her table and set it with plates and tableware. She ate with undisguised hunger, stuffing herself with twice as much as he had thought such a small woman could possibly hold. They talked while they ate.

"So you see," Longarm told her after he sketched in the rough outlines of what had happened in Aurora early in the morning, "there's really more than just Big to worry about. I don't want him gunned down, of course . . . and there's sure to be another reward posted on him now . . . and I don't want anybody else hurt either. If this robbing keeps up, well, other people can be hurt too. I don't want that any more than I want Big hurt."

"What is it you want of me, Custis?"

"Your help," he said bluntly. "I want you to help me find Big and arrest him. For his own protection and everybody else's."

"I've already told you—"

"I know that. But you're the best hope I've got. I mean, I know the man myself, and I've talked to some of his cowboy friends. I know the sort of things he's said in that kind of conversation, and it doesn't give me a clue about where he might be hiding now. But he would have talked about different things with you.

Maybe . . ." He shook his head. "I don't know. I'm grasping at straws. I admit that. What I was hoping was that he might have mentioned something to you. A friend. Someplace that he thinks is pretty. Someplace he goes when he wants to be by himself. Anything like that. It could seem unimportant, but you just never know. Anything might turn out to be the break we need."

"I still do not believe Chester committed those robberies, Custis."

"I know that. But I'd like you to think about it and tell me anything you can remember. Anything at all. It would help Big as much as it would help everybody else."

She frowned and pushed her finally empty plate aside. She gathered the dishes and the leftovers and carried them to the dry sink. Longarm brought in a bucket of fresh water and picked up a dish towel to start drying for her. She was elbow deep in suds.

"You don't have to do that."

"I don't mind." He went on wiping the washed plates and steel tableware.

Miss Hufnagel seemed to be deep in thought. He did not want to disturb her.

Longarm watched her as she busied herself with the routine chores of evening. She was a little bit of a thing. But not unattractive. She certainly wasn't fancy, but she had a good, solid quality about her that said she had come from better than this. She hadn't ever said what it was that brought her to taking in laundry on the edge of Englewood and living hand to mouth.

She finished washing the last fork and handed it to him to dry. A tear was rolling slowly down her cheek.

Longarm laid a hand gently on her shoulder.

Sally Anne began to cry. She came silently to him and pressed her face against his chest. Her shoulders were shuddering and quaking.

"I'm afraid for Chester. I don't want to do anything

66

that would hurt him. But I . . . I'm afraid for those other people too. People I don't even know. I couldn't stand to be responsible for anything happening to someone if I . . . if I could have done anything to stop it. Do you understand, Custis?"

He nodded and wrapped his arms around her, holding her close and offering her what comfort and understanding he could. He stroked her head and the back of her neck and held her silently.

After a while she calmed, and the pattern of her breathing changed. It slowed and deepened and then, unexpectedly, quickened slightly.

He expected her to pull away from him. Instead she pressed herself closer to him and put her arms tight around his waist.

He could feel a subtle change in her posture and responded with the beginnings of an erection.

Sally Anne's belly was pressing tight against his fly. She had to be able to feel his response to her but instead of withdrawing she continued to hold on to him.

"You must think me a terrible hussy," she whispered into his chest.

There was no way a man could agree with a statement like that even if it was so. Longarm ran a hand lightly up and down her back. He was fully hard now, his erection trapped between his body and hers. She wriggled slowly back and forth against it as if relishing the feel of his shaft. Her breath was coming more and more quickly.

Sally Anne tipped her face up to his, and he kissed her. Her kiss was clumsy at first. Then she opened herself to him, and her lips softened and seemed to melt under his.

"Oh, dear. I hadn't . . . I hadn't expected this," she whispered.

"If you'd rather not . . ." He tried to pull away, but she clung to him.

"I do want to. If . . . if you don't mind, that is."

67

He smiled and kissed her again. "Mind? You make the finest offer any woman could give to a man, and you expect me to mind?" He held her tight and stroked her cheek. "I'm honored, Miss Hufnagel." His smile turned into a grin. "But you'll excuse me, I hope, if I don't bow. I don't want to let go of you long enough for that."

She laughed, and some of the tension went out of her slim body. She molded herself to him, and this time when she kissed him it was freely and with a growing fervor.

Longarm picked her up and realized then that he did not know where to carry her.

"Over there. Behind the blanket." Her "bedroom" was a tiny alcove partitioned off from the rest of the one-room shack by a blanket suspended from a rope. He carried her to it.

Her bed was a narrow cot wide enough for only one. Which was entirely adequate at the moment. He lowered her to it and ran his hands lightly up and down her body while her lips worked hungrily against his. Her hunger for closeness seemed every bit as great as her hunger for food had been earlier. Perhaps much greater, in fact.

"You can blow the lamp out so you won't have to look at me," she offered.

"Don't have to . . ." He smiled at her. "I want to see and touch and enjoy every part of you."

"You mean that, don't you."

"Of course I do."

Her answering kiss was fierce, and her hands fumbled for him. She began unfastening the buttons of his fly.

Longarm stopped her. "Wait. There's no hurry. Let me give a little before I take so much." Whatever was in this thin, pained little woman's past it had left her with damned little in the way of self-esteem. He guessed that some dumb son of a bitch had taken much from her

68

sometime in the past. He wanted to give her back at least some of what that idiot had destroyed.

He kissed her again and slowly unbuttoned the bodice of her dress, slipping it down off her shoulders to expose her body to him.

She was skinny, her flesh scant over her ribs. Her breasts were small, tipped with tiny pink nipples. Her belly was sunken and her pelvic bones sharply protruding. Even her thighs were thin.

She turned her head away when he first looked at her, as if she expected him to turn away in revulsion from the sight of her naked body.

Longarm kissed the side of her neck, then her ear. He traced the strong, fine line of her neck with the tip of his tongue and let it play lightly lower. Down across her chest to her left nipple.

He encircled her nipple with his tongue and felt it come erect and hard under the warm, moist touch. Sally Anne gasped.

Her breathing was ragged now, and her hips surged gently up and down as if beyond her power to control.

He suckled softly at her nipple and slipped a hand between her legs.

Sally Anne opened herself to him. She was already wet, he discovered. She began to moan when he slid his hand to caress her more intimately.

He stroked slowly in and out, penetrating only a little at first and then deeper and deeper, a little more each time until she was able to accommodate him.

With the ball of his thumb he found and began to gently massage the tiny button of her pleasure while he continued to suck and pull at first one nipple and then the other.

Sally Anne began to make small, mewling sounds deep in her throat, and her hips pumped to meet his touch. She impaled herself on his fingers.

Her response quickened and grew until she was plunging wildly up and down.

A thin, high-pitched sound began to issue from her tight throat, and her hips bucked faster and faster until with a barely contained scream she shuddered and stiffened in a spasm of wild release.

Her head thrashed back and forth, and the cords of sinew stood out sharp at her throat.

When finally she relaxed it was suddenly and completely.

She fainted dead away, her body falling back against the narrow bed and her head lolling to one side. Her breathing was slow and deep.

Longarm grinned to himself.

Be damned, he thought. Now that didn't happen just every time.

Sally Anne was out cold.

Still grinning, he stood and began to take his clothes off. He wanted to be there beside her when she came around again. And while he was sure as hell willing to give pleasure, he wanted to take a little back for himself too.

He stripped quickly and lay down beside her.

He was there ready with a smile and a kiss when her eyes came open again.

Chapter 14

Sally Anne slipped off the cot, having to climb over Longarm's lean frame to do so, and went to find a discarded tin can for his ashes while he lighted a cheroot and drew the smoke deep into his lungs. He felt satisfied if not quite yet completely satiated. Sally Anne was not all that experienced, but she was damn sure a quick learner. The little woman could give a wild ride indeed.

She came back to the bed and nestled tight against his side, one arm draped possessively across his chest. "Thank you," she said.

"Thank *you*," he responded.

Sally Anne sighed.

She was quiet for a moment, then said, "I wasn't going to help you. But I suppose I have to."

"Mmm?"

"About finding Chester, I mean."

"It's important," he assured her.

"I know it is. Drat it."

Longarm remained quiet and drew on the cheroot. He did not want to push her. She would get to it in her own good time if there was anything she could tell him.

"Mostly Chester liked to talk about horses, even though I know nothing about them. And to tell you the truth, Custis, I care even less than I know. But they were important to him. And really just about all he knew." Her eyes went wide. "Isn't that awful?"

"What, that horses are all Big knows?"

"No. It's awful that I was speaking of Chester in the past tense just then. Like he was already dead." She seemed quite horrified by the lapse that he had not even noticed.

"Well, one of the things I want to do, you know, is make sure you don't have to talk about him dead."

She grimaced and laid her cheek on his chest. "I know that, Custis. I just . . . Anyway, I don't know that I ever heard him mention anything that will help you find him before those awful bounty hunters do. But I've been trying to think back to the things he said when he was here. The only thing I can recall that might possibly help you would be a camp he told me about once." She frowned in concentration as she tried to remember.

"This place . . . let me see if I can get this right, now. This place was in the mountains. Or possibly it was in the foothills. Higher than here, anyway. I am sure of that. He said something about it being green and cool and the grass staying strong after the grass down here was brown and dry. Does that make any sense to you?"

"Yeah, it does." Down on the flat plains where Denver and Englewood were, the grass browned early, by July most years. It took the cooler heights and good water to keep grass green at this time of year. Sally Anne might not know that, but Big Little certainly did.

"He said something about a small ranch there. A place he wished he could work. I asked him if he didn't want a place of his own someday, but he told me no. He knew he wasn't smart enough to run a ranch of his very own. It took a smart man like Mr. Vieren to do that. But someday he would like to work at this ranch in the higher country because it was so pretty there, and all their horses were so pretty. He said . . ." She frowned again in concentration.

"Oh dear, I can't be sure if I remember all this the way Chester said it or not."

"Just do the best you can."

She nodded and let her hand trail down across his stomach. It tickled. She began idly curling strands of

Longarm's pubic hair around the tip of her index finger while she thought.

"He said something about the horses all being so pretty. All of them the same color. Do you remember that when I first met Chester I told him about an article I read? That was when he asked me to teach him to read?"

Longarm nodded.

"Well, the article was about odd colorations in horses. I believe it was during that same conversation that Chester mentioned this little ranch. And wanting to go there someday to work. And if I remember correctly, he said the horses at this place he admired so much were all . . . oh, how did he put it? Bucks? That doesn't make sense, does it? Bucks are deer, aren't they?"

"Buckskin?" Longarm suggested.

"That was it!" Sally Anne sat up abruptly. She forgot, though, that she still had several strands of Longarm's hair twined around her finger. When she snatched her hand away she took the hair with her. He yelped. When he jumped he dislodged hot ash from the cheroot. It fell onto his chest, adding that to the sharp if minor pain down below.

"Oh! Oh, dear. I'm so *sorry*!" She looked stricken with regret. But she couldn't help laughing at the same time. He began to laugh, too, once the hurting stopped.

"I really am sorry, Custis. Honestly I am. But you looked so funny when you jumped like that." She giggled. "I'm sorry, dear." She tried to look contrite and apologetic, but the effect was lost in the intermittent giggles that kept creeping out past her expressions of great concern.

Longarm chuckled and kissed her.

"Do you think it would feel better if I were to kiss it and make it well again?"

"Actually," he said, "I'm fairly sure it would feel a lot better if you did that." He kept his voice dry and his expression deadpan.

She giggled again and winked at him. Sally Anne was not a very good winker. Her other eye drooped halfway shut when she tried to wink.

"It might not help, you know," she said.

Longarm shrugged. "Might not at that." He faked a yawn and looked away with feigned disinterest.

"Darn you."

Sally Anne pouted and smacked him on the chest. Her hand landed flat and hard enough to sting. The sound of it was sharp. Instantly she looked shocked and regretful. "Oh, dear, I've gone and hurt you again."

Longarm laughed. He pulled her down to him and kissed her concerns away.

With a happy sigh, Sally Anne returned his kiss and squirmed inside the tight circle of his arms. After a little while, just when he thought things were getting interesting to the point of no return, she pulled away from him.

"Where d'you think you're going?"

She giggled. "I promised to kiss and make well, didn't I?"

"Mmm, I expect I do recollect something about that, yes."

"Well?"

He laughed. "I wouldn't want to make you break a promise."

Sally Anne chuckled and bent over him.

The girl might've been a slow starter but she came along just fine for the long haul, thank you.

He reached over and dropped the half-smoked cheroot into the can she had brought for him. The cigar wasn't nearly as interesting at the moment as what Sally Anne was doing.

Chapter 15

By the time the sun cleared the eastern horizon, Long-arm had the Circle Y in sight. He'd spent the night with Sally Anne and had gotten an early start when she rose to start her fires for the day's work.

The tip she had given him about a ranch where buck-skins were raised was interesting enough to follow, but neither Sally Anne nor Longarm knew where Big's dream ranch was supposed to be.

Pat Vieren might know. Besides, Longarm wanted to talk to Pat anyway. And, probably more important, to Pat's hired hand, Tom Lee. Tom had shared the bunk-house with Big since Tom came to work on the Circle Y, and a man tends to say things about himself in the night hours when he's waiting for sleep. Longarm had in-tended to make the Circle Y his next stop after seeing Sally Anne anyway.

At this hour, well into the dawning, breakfast at the Circle Y would be long since over and done with, so Longarm ignored the curl of smoke from Althea Vieren's chimney and rode on toward the barns. He could see a horse's ears bobbing in and out of view on the other side of a breaking pen fence, so Pat or Tom or the both of them should be there. The walls of the pen, built tight so a young horse would not be distracted from the business at hand by looking at things outside the "office," kept Long-arm from seeing who it was he was approaching.

He rode up beside the round pen—it was a common enough breaking arrangement, with a rounded shape and a snubbing post set deep into the ground smack in the middle of the circle—and stopped his rented horse there.

There was no sign of Pat. Tom Lee stood beside the snubbing post with a lunge line in one hand and a short whip in the other. He was putting a sleek-bodied young stallion, about a two-year-old, through its gaits. The horse, a leggy plantation walker from the looks of it, had a swift, proud trot and a fine headset that it was demonstrating when Longarm got there. The slanting sunlight gleamed on its sleek coat as firm muscles rippled beneath its skin.

The horse trotted around the circle, then caught sight of Longarm's chest and shoulders above the wall as it rounded toward him. It threw its head and boogered, spinning over its hocks and thundering back the way it had just come.

"Whoa, you son of a bitch, whoa." Lee hauled in some slack in the lunge line and jerked, pulling the young horse's head around and bringing it to a trembling, nostril-flaring stop. "What the hell'd you go an' do that for, damn you?" Lee complained.

"My fault," Longarm apologized.

"What? Oh. It's you, Marshal. I didn't see you there."

"*He* did. Sorry I spooked him."

Lee nodded.

Longarm swung down from the saddle and tied the livery gelding to a post, then found the gate and went inside the breaking pen.

The young stud was calm again. Lee had called it to him and was switching the lunge clip from one side of the horse's halter to the other so he could work it in the other direction. "If you're looking for Pat . . ." he said over his shoulder.

"I am, but I wanted to talk to you too, Tom."

"Sure." Lee rubbed the stallion's velvety muzzle and let the horse drift on its own for a moment. He leaned against the snubbing post and fished inside his shirt pocket for a twist of tobacco.

Tom Lee was a middling sized man but built on the narrow side. He was bowlegged enough to make the ladies think he'd been born in a saddle, but Longarm had heard him mention something about a boyhood in Philadelphia. He had a straggly mustache and always seemed to need a shave or a haircut or both, but Pat said he had a good touch with horses and was reliable except for payday drunks. Longarm knew the man, although not well. Tom had come to work for Pat four or five months earlier. Other than the one remark about Philadelphia and the mention of a few California place names, he didn't say much about himself.

Longarm joined him in leaning against the stout post and nipped the end off a cheroot. He didn't offer one to Tom because by then Lee was already chewing. The chestnut colt took advantage of the break to lie down in the sandy loam and treat himself to a roll. Longarm thought the horse was a little light in the chest to make a good stud. But of course he wasn't going to express an opinion on the subject. A decision like that was Pat's to make, and an unsolicited opinion could cause hard feelings.

Tom Lee was watching the horse too. "That 'un won't make it," he said.

"No?"

"Naw. Pat bred him once this year to see what he'd fetch. Damn shame to lose the blood line, fancy as it is. But my money says the sonuvabitch won't throw any better'n he is. Pat'll end up gelding 'im before next season." He turned his head and spat. "I expect I know what's brought you here, Marshal."

"I expect you do, Tom."

"Wish I could tell you somethin'. But I sure as hell don't know where ol' Big could've took off to. Racked my brain about it, I have, but I come up empty." He grinned and spat again. "Funny how I do that so much when I try an' think."

Longarm smiled. "Hell, I thought I was the only one with that problem."

"Seriously, Marshal, I just can't think o' nothing Big

77

ever said that might help. Sure did surprise me t' hear about him. I never figured him for that kind. You know?"

"I know," Longarm agreed.

"Yeah, sure was a surprise. You never know though, right?"

"No, you never know." Longarm drew on his cheroot and tipped his hat forward against the slant of the sun. "Did you even know Big had a gun?"

"Oh, I knew he owned one, if that's what you mean. I seen it a time or two. But Big never carried it. Never played with it or cleaned it, hardly. You know how some guys are. All the time messing with a gun if they own one. Big never done that. In fact, I never seen the thing outside the bunkhouse an' that not more than once or twice. An' I never paid attention to it. I mean, a lot o' guys own guns. Some outfits most guys do. So I never thought anything of it. I mean, you know yourself how Big was. Gentle, or so I thought."

"Yeah, I know."

"So I never thought anything about it."

"He never said anything to you about wanting to pull a robbery?"

"Hell, no. I'd've told Pat right off if he done that. I mean, we lived in the same place an' I suppose you could say we was friends. But we wasn't bosom buddies, if you know what I mean. We kinda went our own way in town mostly. He liked t' go to Englewood mostly. I generally go t' Denver when I want a night on the town. Wasn't a hard an' fast rule with neither of us, an' sometimes we went in together. But mostly not."

Longarm nodded and examined the ash that was lengthening on the tip of his cheroot. "Did Big ever mention anyplace, a ranch maybe, that he particularly favored?"

"Not that I recall."

"Maybe someplace where they raise buckskin horses?"

"No . . ." Lee started, then paused. "Now wait a min-

78

ute. I don't recall Big ever talking special 'bout such a place, but I think I know where you mean."

Longarm's interest quickened.

"I had t' deliver a filly there. Just after I come here, that was. Pat had sold this yearlin' filly, a *bayo coyote* she was, an' the critter had to be delivered. If I remember right, Big was hopin' to do that himself but he was down sick that day. Had an ache in his chest an' a sore throat, like, and Miz Vieren made him stay in bed the whole day an' wouldn't let him go. So Pat had me take the filly."

"*Bayo coyote*, you say?"

"That's right. Pretty little thing, too. Real nice head on her."

Longarm added Texas to Tom Lee's past. It wasn't always what a man said outright that told such things on him, but his riding gear or the expressions he used in conversation. *Bayo coyote*, for instance. It was a Texas cow-country term for what would be called a lineback dun in most parts of the West. "So where was this place you delivered the filly?"

"Ranch owned by a man name of Sawyer. Bert? Benny? Something like that. Sawyer, anyhow. It's in the foothills just south o' Boulder. I expect I could find it again, though I'm not so sure I'd remember good enough to give anybody else directions to it. Pat could tell you, o' course. He's the one told me how to find it. Rode one horse an' led the filly. Time we got there she was broke to lead pretty good." He grinned and winked. "First time she'd been off the place, an' I guess she was nervous. Had us a fine ol' time to start with. I bet she went the first two miles walkin' on her back legs an' squealin' an' carrying on. She got the hang of it after a bit an' settled down. Good little horse, she's gonna be." He turned his head and spat.

The two-year-old stallion who soon would be a three-year-old gelding wandered over and sniffed at Longarm's belly. Its breath tickled. It got a whiff of gunpowder or something else it didn't recognize, snorted a spray of snot onto his vest and trousers and whirled around to scamper as far away as the pen walls would permit. Within seconds, though, it was sneaking back for another sniff. A horse is every bit as curious as a dog and just as dependent on its sense of smell to decide what it likes and what it doesn't.

Longarm grinned and ignored the dampness on his clothes. The colt was pretending complete disinterest in this visitor but was sidling toward him again ever so slowly while trying to look like it wasn't.

With Big Little and a gang of postal robbers still wandering loose in the brush, though, this was no time to be playing with youngsters, two legged or four. Longarm dropped the remains of his cheroot into the dirt and ground it out underfoot. "Thanks for your help, Tom."

"Wish I could do more for you, Marshal."

"A man can't tell what he doesn't know."

"No, I reckon that's true enough."

"Where'd you say I could find Pat?" He needed to have a word with Vieren and get directions to this Sawyer spread south of Boulder. Then damn sure get on the way there.

He was already figuring the quickest way. Riding directly there would take too long. Better, he decided, to take the livery horse to Denver and load it and himself on a train for Boulder, then ride down from there. Or take a train to Golden and ride north, depending on just where Vieren said the place was.

"Pat's in the house doing bookwork, I think."

Longarm grunted softly to himself. "Thanks, Tom."

"Any time, Marshal."

Chapter 16

Byron Sawyer was a man in his mid-fifties or thereabouts, with steel-gray hair and a closely trimmed mustache. He looked fit and healthy enough to keep going for another fifty years or so, and had built his place as if he expected to be using it that much longer.

The Sawyer outfit—the Bar Horseshoe Bar according to a brand burnt into the gateposts Longarm had just passed—was situated in a lovely little bowl high in the foothills. A cold, burbling stream ran through the middle of the tiny valley, and the grass on both sides was lush and green. The hillsides were forested with fir, and there were thick stands of quaking aspen where the hills and the grass met.

From the ranch yard a man could look out over the pale, rolling plains for what seemed a hundred miles or more. It was a hell of a pretty sight out there, and the ranch buildings were just as pretty in a much different way.

The buildings were stoutly constructed, and it was apparent that care had been put into both their building and their placement. From the porch of Sawyer's house a man could see forever toward the plains, and the mountains rose majestic and protecting at his back.

Carefully fenced haystacks were large and lush green near the barns, and a heard of forty or fifty sleek buckskin horses, mares with a flock of youngsters at their heels, were lazing on the bright grass near the stream.

Longarm was impressed with the outfit and with the owner alike.

Sawyer was in his shirtsleeves and had a napkin

tucked under his collar like a bib when he answered Longarm's knock.

When Longarm introduced himself, Sawyer's welcome was warm and immediate.

"Come inside, Marshal. You're just in time to take dinner with us. We can talk while we eat."

"Thanks." Longarm wasn't about to refuse. He hadn't gotten around to eating yet today, unless a lump of dough that was trying to pass as a sweet bun could be called eating. He'd bought that at the railroad depot in Denver and choked it down while he was busy writing out a note for a boy to carry to the Federal Building telling Billy where Longarm was and why.

Mrs. Sawyer was as welcoming as her husband. There were two grown "boys" at the table who were introduced to the guest as the Sawyer sons. Mrs. Sawyer laid another place quickly for the unexpected company and insisted on heaping Longarm's plate with pork chops and fried potatoes and freshly baked bread. There was a pie cooling on a trivet beside Byron Sawyer's plate. Longarm was almighty glad he had timed his visit so nicely.

"Now, what is it brings us the pleasure of your company?" Sawyer asked when Longarm was comfortably ensconced behind a mound of food.

"I was hoping you could help me locate a fella named Big Little. Do you know him?"

Sawyer frowned for a moment in thought. "The name sure rings a bell. Give me a second." He smiled. "Sure I do. Great big fella? Supposed to be some hand with horses? Works for Pat Vieren down on the flatlands?"

"That's him," Longarm agreed.

"Sure, I remember him now. Nice man. He's been up here, oh, two or three times delivering horses I've bought off Pat, and I've talked to him down there too when I've been looking at Pat's stock. Of course I remember him. He even told me once he'd like to work for me here. But of course long as the boys stay with me I won't need any hired help, and I expect them to stick around and inherit when the time comes. We make enough of a living for all of us if we don't get greedy. Which is what I told Little." He nodded, as if confirming his own memories now that he had gotten them started. "Sure, I remember him now. Nice man."

"Whatever would you want with Mr. Little, Marshal?" Mrs. Sawyer asked.

When he told them she grabbed up her apron and lifted it to cover her face. "No!"

"Yes, ma'am, I'm afraid so." He turned to Sawyer. "You hadn't heard about the post office shootings?"

"No, we don't get to town much and don't see a newspaper one month to the next usually." Sawyer clucked loudly and shook his head. "To think of it, though. A man we know, doing something like that. And he did seem such a nice fellow too."

The younger Sawyers leaned forward with quick interest and wanted to press the deputy for all the gory details. They were disappointed, though. Longarm did not want to deliver any, certainly not with their mother listening. She seemed quite shocked enough without that.

"I take it you haven't seen Big lately?"

Sawyer shook his head. "Not since the last time I visited Pat at the Circle Y," he said. "I bought a filly from him. Nice little horse, too, which all Pat's stock always are. He knows how to breed, that man does. I'm sure I saw Little when I was down there, but another man delivered her to us. It wasn't Little that trip."

"Tom Lee," Longarm said. He noticed one of the boys making a face and asked about it.

"Aw, nothin' really. I just didn't like him so much as I did Mr. Little. He'd been drinking and was bragging about . . . well, you know what I mean. I was worried Ma might hear. That's all."

"You liked Little, though?"

83

"Sure. He was always fun to talk to. Always had a story to tell, and he could get you to laughing so your belly hurt."

That was Big all right, Longarm agreed. "Did Little ever tell stories about highwaymen and gun fights and stuff like that?" He himself couldn't remember ever hearing Big talk about things like that. Mostly just about horses and people he had known before. But then a man wouldn't necessarily talk about other things if he had a past and knew there was a federal deputy close by. It was something that hadn't occurred to Longarm to ask of anyone before.

"No, sir, but I remember one he told on himself once about a sore-backed pack mule and a Mexican cook down along the Pecos when . . ."

Longarm chuckled. He'd heard Big tell that same story, and it was a good one.

It was also one that shouldn't be told in front of a fella's mother. The other Sawyer boy shushed his brother.

"But none of you has seen Little lately?"

"No, I can't say that we have. Mother?"

She shook her head.

"No, sir," each of the boys added. "Not for quite a while."

Longarm frowned. He'd been halfway sure he would find Big here.

But, damnit, if these good people were lying to him, they were sure getting away with it. Everything about them said they were telling him the truth. They certainly did not act like anyone with something to hide. They seemed open and honest and genuinely concerned.

If the Sawyer family was sitting there feeding him and lying to him then probably he should turn in his badge quick before Billy got around to firing him again, permanently this time and for good reason. Because he damn sure believed them.

It was always possible, of course, that Big could

have headed this way and be holed up in the hills some-where close by simply because he favored the area so much. But surely Byron Sawyer or one of his boys would have spotted him or signs of him if that was so.

He asked, but again they had nothing to tell him. They hadn't seen Big or any signs of any unknown bummers camping in the vicinity.

"I wish we could help you, Marshal. And to tell you the truth, I hope when you do find whoever did those things that it turns out Mr. Little wasn't part of it. He surely did seem a nice man. I'd hate to think that any-one we know and liked could've done a hateful thing like shoot two people."

"Yes, sir," Longarm said noncommitally. Unfortu-nately for that clerk at the Aurora post office, Longarm himself had once harbored the same false hope. Long-arm didn't even know yet if the clerk was alive or dead.

He allowed the unpleasant subject to drop and con-centrated on the dinner Mrs. Sawyer had prepared. It was the best meal he'd had in ages, and he piled com-pliments as deep as she had piled his plate.

The pie turned out to be rhubarb, crusty with sugar and tart enough to make a man wish for as many stom-achs as a cow so he could hold more of it.

Chapter 17

Longarm waved good-bye and reined away from the Sawyer place with a feeling of warm well-being in his stomach but of disquiet otherwise.

He had been putting perhaps too much hope on finding Big Little at the Sawyer ranch. He still did not, though, believe that the Sawyers lied to him. They seemed open, honest folk with nothing to gain or to hide by bringing a murderer into their midst and concealing him from the law.

He jogged the livery horse into motion and wound down along the stream that led out toward the plains from the Bar Horseshoe Bar.

The afternoon sun was hot on his back, and a light breeze was welcome when it spilled down over the white dotted but nearly bare peaks behind and slid past him on its way to the flat grasslands ahead.

Longarm removed his tweed coat, folded it and turned in the saddle to secure it behind the cantle of his worn old McClellan.

"Damn," he muttered as one rein slithered out of his grasp and down over the withers of the horse. He left the coat attached by a single set of strings and bent to retrieve the fallen rein before the gelding stepped on it.

A sound like that of a hornet droning at high speed crossed above his head.

Longarm blanched and leaned over further, the dropped rein out of mind now. He kicked free of the stirrups and dropped to the ground, landing lightly on all fours and scuttling to the side.

Before he hit the ground he heard the hollow yap of

the gunshot from somewhere off to his left as the sound caught up with the bullet.

The horse bogged its head and bolted forward on the road, Longarm's coat flapping loose as the animal bucked and snorted in its sudden terror.

Longarm by then was throwing himself sideways, crabbing quickly and low to the ground toward the meager cover offered by a hillock of gravel and grass. There were no rocks or boulders nearby to get behind, and he went for the best that was available.

A second slug tore into the earth between him and the cover, sending a spray of dirt and gravel high into the air. The deformed slug whined nastily off into the distance as it ricocheted off the ground.

Longarm threw himself forward into the shelter of the scant cover, rolled and came up with his Colt in hand. His Winchester was still uselessly in its scabbard on the horse that by now was disappearing into a swale at a hard, belly-down run.

A puff of faint, pale smoke hung for a moment at the base of an aspen clump up the slope Longarm faced. It shifted in the air there, then was whipped away by the breeze.

Longarm had no good target, only a general area to shoot at. He took careful aim beside the bole of a thick aspen trunk and squeezed off a shot.

Answering fire and smoke lanced toward him from beside the tree next to the one where he had been aiming. He ducked reflexively and cussed a little under his breath. He'd shot at the wrong damned mark. The puff of muzzle smoke must have drifted a few feet before he spotted it that first time.

The rifleman's bullet sizzled through the air above him and thumped to earth somewhere behind. The guy was aiming too high. It was a common mistake on downhill shots. Longarm did not feel inclined to give the son of a bitch lessons on how to do better.

He fired again, the big Thunderer bucking in his hand, this time aiming beside the right tree.

There was no yelp or screech of pain, and he had no way of knowing if his shot connected or not. He cocked the Colt, foregoing the double-action mechanism in favor of the lighter pull and better trigger control of a single-action shot, took careful aim and fired a third round.

A chip of bark flew from the side of the aspen, sailed high into the air and then fluttered back down to earth.

From somewhere deep in the aspen clump a piñon jay squawled its rasping, raucous call and fluttered into motion above the treetops.

The jay could have been startled into motion by a fleeing ambusher.

Or the bird might just have taken a notion to head for new ground. The rifleman could still be lying there waiting for Longarm to show himself.

Longarm hesitated.

If the guy was flushed and running, this would be the time to charge up the hill after him.

On the other hand, if the damned bird took off for its own reasons, showing himself would be as good as asking the ambusher to dye his shirtfront red. With blood.

Longarm was hardly a timid sort. But he liked to think that he wasn't a stupid sort either. And charging an entrenched rifleman while carrying nothing better than a revolver was stupid indeed.

He decided on discretion and triggered another shot toward the place where he had last seen gunfire, then hunched lower to the ground and rolled onto his side to quickly reload the Colt.

"Shit," he mumbled aloud.

Long, silent minutes crawled by without incident. Maybe the bastard had been running. Maybe Longarm had given up a chance to charge him. And maybe Martin Luther was the pope's favorite author, too. Longarm wasn't inclined to count on either idea.

The sun, so warm just a few minutes earlier, seemed to have lost its strength now. The wind coming off the mountains into Longarm's face seemed chill and unwelcoming. He wished he had his damn coat.

He grunted softly to himself and shifted to his right, to the very edge of the hillock he was hiding behind.

A wink of light and a puff of smoke from the left edge of the aspens sent him rolling for cover again.

The bullet found gravel instead of flesh, but the son of a bitch had corrected his aim. This time the slug landed in front of the lump of earth that was Longarm's shield. Bits of dirt and stone rained over his hat and shirt. Better that than lead.

Longarm popped up and triggered two quick shots toward the place where the bastard had been, but he had little hope the guy was still there. He swung the muzzle of the Thunderer to the right and sent a pair of searching shots close to the ground where he thought the rifleman might have rolled, then dropped close to the ground and reloaded again.

A frown crossed his face. Much of his loose ammunition was in the side pocket of his coat. Wherever that was. There was more in his saddlebags. Wherever they were. He cussed a little and reminded himself it might not be a bad idea to conserve his shots. This could turn out to be a longer siege than he expected. And poor as a revolver is against a rifle, it sure as hell beat a pocket-knife.

He inched forward again to where he could see the aspens again.

A magpie flying up from the south tucked its wings and darted toward the aspens, then suddenly flared toward the sky and flew back the way it had come.

Was the guy moving now? Was he running? There was no way to tell. The jay had lied earlier. Why not the magpie now?

Longram wriggled to his left, butt down and belt buckle dragging. A right-handed man normally shoots from the right side of a barrier. That would be where the rifleman would be watching.

If the guy was watching.

Longarm took a fresh grip on the Colt and lay in the glare of the sunlight waiting and watching with stolid patience.

"Marshal? Is that you, Marshal?"

"Careful. There could be a guy still in those trees."

Byron Sawyer motioned, and his boys reined their mounts up the slope toward the aspen trees with their innocently fluttering leaves.

"Nothing up here, Papa. We don't see nothing at all."

With a disgusted frown, Longarm stood and brushed off his shirtfront and trousers.

Sawyer and his boys were riding handsome, muscular young buckskins. None of the three of them was armed with so much as a shotgun.

"You all right, Marshal?" Sawyer pulled his horse to a stop on the road.

Longarm nodded, still disgusted. "Yeah, damnit, I'm all right."

"We heard shooting," Sawyer said.

"Ambush." Longarm gave the horse breeder a cold look. "Just as I was leaving your place."

Sawyer did not react like a man who was guilty of anything. He swung off his saddle and ground reined the buckskin. "Bubba? Joey? Do you see anything at all up there?"

The boys dismounted and began kicking through the litter of old leaves. Longarm and their father walked up the slope to join them. The rifleman had been a little more than a hundred yards from the road when he fired. Not quite close enough. Whoever the guy was, he wasn't much of a shot. Any man halfway adept with a rifle should be able to keep his shots inside a pie plate at that range, downhill or not. A really good shot with a good rifle should be able to plink teacups at the distance. Or heads. Longarm was grateful for the favor.

"Here's something," one of the boys said. He bent and retrieved a shiny brass cartridge case, then another.

Longarm thought for a moment, then said, "There should be four of them."

The boys poked through the limp, dead aspen leaves on the ground until they had accounted for all four empties. The cartridge cases were common .44-40s, the most ordinary and unremarkable of calibers anywhere west of the Atlantic Ocean. Whoever the would-be killer was, Longarm was not going to spot him by his choice of weapon.

Longarm grunted and bent to retrieve something the boys had overlooked in the ground litter. Cigar butts. Two of them. Each smoked down to a nubbin.

"Been long since you've had a rain or snow flurries?" he asked. At this altitude one could get snow at almost any time of year.

Byron Sawyer thought for a moment. "Week, ten days?" He gave his sons a questioning look. Each of them nodded. "About that," one of them said.

The question had been mostly rhetorical, anyway. Longarm was curious about the Sawyers' reaction more than their answer. Not only were the cigar butts dry, the ash that clung to their tips was powdery and fresh. They hadn't lain exposed more than a few hours at the most.

The unseen rifleman had been lying in wait here for some time, and he smoked while he was here. Two cigars' worth of time. How long would that be? More than an hour unless he was awfully nervous. Possibly several hours.

Longarm reached for a cheroot, then realized his smokes were wherever the runaway horse had gotten to. They were in his coat, damnit.

The cigar butts, though, considerably reduced his suspicions that the Sawyers could have set him up for an ambush. He had spent a fair amount of time with them at their home, and he had seen none of them smoke, nor were there any signs of smoking anywhere in the house. No pipes or humidors. No ashtrays in the parlor. He sifted through his impressions inside the Sawyer house and came up with nothing.

And he knew damned good and well none of them had been lying here for any hour waiting to ambush him since he had just left them and their mother at the ranch before he started down.

Probably it had been . . . he thought back . . . two hours or more since he had ridden this road toward the Bar Horseshoe Bar and stopped there for lunch and a long talk. Call it two hours. The ambusher could have been waiting here for him nearly all that time, then.

So how the hell had the rifleman known he would be passing this way?

Lucky guess? Sure. With all of northeastern Colorado to choose from, the guy picked this spot at this moment to wait for a shot at a U.S. deputy marshal.

The guy hadn't been at the Sawyer place when Longarm got there. Longarm almost certainly would have seen him riding out toward his ambush site.

He'd been holed up somewhere on the slopes near the Sawyer place and saw Longarm ride by? Much more likely. Even though the Sawyers hadn't particularly noticed anyone camping in the neighborhood, it did not necessarily follow that Big and his gang weren't hiding in the hills around here. It might only mean that the Sawyers didn't see them. But then the Sawyers hadn't been looking for anyone either. Just tending to their stock, mostly on their own land, more than likely. So it was entirely possible that the gang's hole-up was somewhere on these slopes immediately above where Longarm and the Sawyers were standing at this moment.

He walked around to the side of the aspen clump and stared up toward the hills that from here rose quickly and abruptly to the peaks.

Big and his gang could be somewhere up there staring back at him this instant.

But if they were, damnit, he couldn't see them.

He frowned and went back to join the Sawyer men.

"I'd appreciate it if one of you could ride up the road there and see if you can spot my horse. It— Wait a minute."

There was dust rising from the road in the swale where Longarm last saw the disappearing ass end of the runaway. A moment later a group of familiar riders crested the near side of the depression and came into view.

They were leading Longarm's riderless horse with them and seemed in something of a hurry.

"Up here," Longarm shouted. He waved his arms to draw their attention. "Up here, Billy."

Chapter 18

There were three riders: Billy Vail and two men Long-arm did not know, but who were wearing badges pinned to their vests. One of the locals was leading Longarm's horse. Billy Vail had Longarm's coat thrown over his pommel.

"I take it you're all right?" Billy asked.

Longarm nodded and quickly explained.

Vail grunted. "We found the horse running loose on the road. I thought the rig looked like yours. The coat was up the way a half mile or so. Then I knew it was you in trouble."

"Damn near in trouble." Longarm got a cheroot from his coat pocket and made some introductions. The ones he got in return disclosed that the marshal's companions were two deputies from Boulder.

"When I got your note about following a lead up here I decided you might need some help," Billy said. "It looks like you did."

"Ayuh. I suppose I did."

"Any idea where they are now?"

Longarm looked toward the hills looming tall to the west. "Somewhere up there, I'd say. They must have a camp where they could keep watch on the road."

One of the local officers, a man named Phister, nod-ded. "We'll find it."

"They'll likely be gone by the time you do."

"Could be, but we'll put a posse together an' make sure. If they're up there, we'll find where they are, or anyhow where they was. We got some men know this country pretty good."

"We'll join you," Sawyer volunteered quickly. "Bubba, ride back to the house and fetch some carbines."

"I'll go with you, and we can get started from there. John, you ride back to town and get some people together. You can start from that end, an' we'll sweep 'em from both sides. If they spot one group an' try to turn back we'll squeeze 'em."

The deputy named John grinned and wheeled his horse back up the road.

"How 'bout you, Marshal?" Phister asked Vail.

"I'll go back to Denver. This is the sort of thing you can do better than I can. You know the ground. We don't."

We. The implication clearly was that Billy Vail wanted Longarm to return to Denver with him.

"Something up, Billy?"

"I would damn sure say there was," Vail told him. "We'll talk about it on the way back."

Which meant it was something Billy wanted to tell. But not where outsiders would be listening in. Otherwise he would spit it out here and now. And otherwise, normal procedure would be for Longarm and probably Billy too—the marshal was no shrinking violet who preferred paperwork and administration to the action of the field—to join the posse. Billy had been one hell of a fine field officer himself before he accepted the appointment that put him behind a desk, and he was normally eager for any excuse that would take him out of the office and into action.

Longarm knew better than to question his boss on the subject right now.

Instead he reclaimed the reins of his horse, tied his coat—securely this time—behind the cantle, and swung into the McClellan.

Bubba Sawyer was already out of sight on his way to fetch weapons for the sweep into the hills from this end, and John was already heading for Boulder to start a crowd down from that end.

Longarm would damn sure have liked to be with them. But this just wasn't the time to be bringing up preferences. "Ready when you are," he said.

He followed Billy up the road toward Boulder and the rail connection back to Denver.

Chapter 19

"You've gotten your ass in a sling," Billy Vail said softly when they were well out of the hearing of the others. They were riding side by side at a slow walk on the narrow road.

"So what else is new?" Longarm turned to fumble inside his coat and find another cheroot.

"No, I mean it this time, Longarm," Billy said. "Mack Bowen was popular with the people who count around here. His friends are getting a letter-writing campaign together. They want to set up a howl in Washington. And at least two state senators are talking about a legislative request that you be removed from duty. Very formal stuff. Both houses of the legislature and an endorsement by the governor, then on to Washington." Vail sighed. "I take it you haven't seen the newspapers today?"

Longarm shook his head. "I've had more important things to do. Hell, you know that, Billy."

"Take my advice then, Longarm. Don't read today's newspapers. Or tomorrow's, for all I know. They . . . are not kind. You refusing to arrest Little when you had the chance . . ." He shrugged. "It's almost like they think you caused the problem. At least you are quick becoming the only readily available whipping boy they have. You're mentioned in editorial comments in both papers already, and unless I don't know these people as well as I think I do, you'll soon be the leading theme in their letters columns too."

Longarm gnawed on the tip of his cheroot. "I'm sorry, Billy. I know they have to burn their way through you if they want to scorch me. I didn't mean to bring anything like that onto you, and I'm sorry."

"What I'm saying, I guess, is that it would be nice if we could relieve the pressure before it reaches Washington and starts back this way from that end. We need a pop valve, Longarm. We need something to let the steam out."

"We need an arrest," Longarm observed.

"As a matter of fact, yes."

They rode along in a silence that was more brooding than companionable, each man deep into his own thoughts and concerns.

Longarm damn sure hadn't intended to put this kind of heat on Billy Vail when he, entirely on his own, decided to investigate further and leave Big Little free the other day.

The error had been his, damnit, but the problem had quickly become Billy's.

Not that Billy was bitching. It wasn't like him to bellyache. Or to go into detail about how this problem was beginning to affect his career.

But damnit, if it wasn't serious Billy wouldn't even be mentioning it. Billy Vail was no nervous Nelly ready to throw his deputies to the wolves at the first sign of disapproval from the bigwigs. He'd proven that time and time again over the years.

Billy Vail would stand behind his people until his boots were filled with blood from all the stab wounds in his back.

But United States marshals were political appointees. No matter how you wanted to slice the cake, they were appointed to their posts and served at the discretion of the people back in Washington, no matter if those Washington political hacks were a bunch of ignorant bastards with big bellies and more charm than common sense.

If the complaints coming out of Denver were so strong now that Billy was mentioning them, then they were strong enough that they could lead not only to Custis Long's dismissal but to Billy Vail's as well.

Longarm felt all the worse for thinking that he might not only have fucked up his own job, but might be costing Billy his as well.

"Damnit, Billy, I'm sorry," he repeated as they came in sight of Boulder.

"There would be one good way to silence them," Billy suggested.

"Yeah. Don't I know it," Longarm said unhappily.

Billy didn't have to tell him what that "one good way" happened to be.

Longarm needed to find Big Little and pin Big's ears to the wall.

He had to find Big and his gang and bring them all in.

Dead or alive, it wouldn't make any difference.

He needed to bring them in and parade them through the streets of Denver, preferably past the gold-domed Capitol Building so all the asshole politicians could see for themselves that their U.S. marshal was doing the job he was paid for.

They had to be marched past in cuffs or dragged past in boxes, the big bellies wouldn't care. But they had to be there, or Billy Vail could well lose his badge right along with Custis Long.

Longarm frowned. "I have a suggestion, boss."

Billy grunted.

"Fire me."

The unusually solemn marshal's pink-cheeked face split into a go-to-hell grin. "Did that already."

"So I recollect. But I'm serious, Billy. You got to fire me. Again."

Vail shook his head. "Thanks for the offer, but it's too late for that." He continued to grin. "You see, I, uh, made a small mistake of my own."

Longarm raised an eyebrow.

"That SOB Parkhurst . . . you know him, don't you?"

"Uh-huh. I know him." Longarm made a face. Leonidas Parkhurst was an aide to the governor who fancied himself a powerful man in Colorado politics. And, hell, maybe he was. He had the ear of a good majority of the elected officials in the state and was a popular ass kisser in Washington too. Rumor had it that he would be running for the state attorney general's position come the next elections and start to build a heady career of his own after years of sucking up to others in high office.

"Parkhurst dropped by to see me this morning. He, um, started off by telling me what I was going to have to do. And you know how I like that." Billy grinned again. So did Longarm. Billy Vail wasn't much for allowing himself to be pushed around.

Longarm drew rein and stopped his horse in the middle of the road. So did Billy. They were just about to the depot, and there would be too many ears in the woodwork once they arrived there.

Vail chuckled softly. "You know how Parkhurst can be. Overbearing son of a bitch. He started to bluster and bully and I guess, um, I guess I threw him out of the office. Sort of."

"You didn't."

The chuckle turned into a rumbling laugh. "I did."

Longarm roared.

"You should have seen the look on his face."

"But you didn't . . ."

Billy nodded. "But I did. By the coat collar and the seat of his britches. Big as he is, it's a wonder I got away with it. I think he was so startled that the unthinkable was happening that he didn't know what was going on until it was too late. Henry saw us coming and snatched the door open, and there went old Parkhurst into the hall and onto his fat butt." Billy doubled over with laughter. "To make it all the better, if that's possible, there was a delegation of suffragists coming down the hall at the time. After they got over being shocked, they thought it was the funniest thing they'd ever seen."

And no wonder, Longarm realized. Leonidas Park-hurst was a firm and sometimes nasty opponent of the women's suffrage movement in the state. The ladies must have gotten a hell of a kick out of seeing one of their prime enemies on his ass in a public hallway.

"Poor Parkhurst was so shaken I don't think he knew whether to piss his pants or punch me. He looked at me and then at the ladies and jumped up and ran for the door like he'd been shot out of a gun." Billy was laughing so hard he was making his horse nervous.

"But jeez, Billy."

"Yeah. Yeah, I know." Billy fished a handkerchief out and dabbed at his eyes with it. The laughter subsided into chuckling rumbles. "Yeah."

Longarm couldn't help laughing with his old friend at the thought of Leonidas Parkhurst flying out through that door. But Lordy, this was serious.

If Longarm didn't do something, and do it damned quick, to take the heat off, Billy Vail was through as United States Marshal for the Denver District.

And all because of *him*.

That was enough to sober anybody.

Longarm headed on toward the depot in silence. There was no point in making promises or grand pronouncements. Talk wasn't going to pull the dogs off this trail. It was going to take some performance to accomplish that. He turned to look back toward the mountains where the locals were by now engaged in their search for Big and his band of post office robbers. Longarm wondered if he should get up there and join them.

The news that was waiting for them at the railroad telegraph office made up his mind about that.

Chapter 20

Another post office had been hit, this one in Broomfield, a small community on the rail line between Denver and Boulder.

Information about the robbery was sketchy. The hastily transmitted wire from Broomfield said only that it had happened. Local officers were asked to be on the alert for a gang of five robbers who fled from Broomfield on horseback after hitting the post office there.

Billy Vail cursed. "I must have passed them on my way up."

"And we've gone and pulled all the locals off to search for them in the hills where they just shot at me, damnit," Longarm added. "Or one of them did. Five robbers, that wire says. We know where the sixth guy was, don't we?"

Billy cussed again.

Longarm started to ask about the next train that would be moving down toward Boulder, but Billy stopped him. "Forget the train. We have an idea where they've been holing up. We'll cut across country from here and try to get ahead of them. With luck . . ."

He didn't have to finish the thought. It would take luck, and plenty of it, for the two of them to intercept a gang riding from Broomfield for the mountains. They had to try it, though. Even though there were literally thousands of square miles and innumerable routes the gang could choose to follow in their flight from Broomfield into the foothills.

All Billy and Longarm could do was ride out onto the

flats and hope to spot some dust rising that would point to the robbers.

"Let's go."

They mounted and fogged it south again, angling this time not along the road toward the Bar Horseshoe Bar but out onto the broad expanse of rolling land that lay between Broomfield and the mountains.

"There," Longarm said. He dropped his cigar butt and ground it out under the heel of his boot before he picked up his reins. Billy Vail was mounted and ready before him.

The two of them had ridden hard for an hour, then chose a promontory from which they could keep watch over as much land as possible.

After a half hour of silent surveillance they were rewarded now with the sight of dust rising from a coulee four miles or more southeast of their lookout.

"Going in the right direction," Billy said, "and moving fast."

"Raising a hell of a cloud too."

Billy grunted. This far out from Broomfield . . . There was no point in speculating about it. The only way they would know for sure would be to cut in front of the riders and stop them.

It would not have occurred to either of them to worry about the fact that there were five robbers riding with the gang today and two peace officers to stop them. By the ordinary odds of the business, the marshals had the gang outnumbered.

"We'll wait for them there," Billy said, pointing toward an oasislike thicket of wild plum off to the south. It was the place Longarm himself would have chosen. Based on the speed they were now traveling at, the distant riders should reach that point in a half hour or a little less. Unless they changed direction. Longarm and Billy could get there in fifteen or twenty minutes riding at a speed that would raise little or no dust.

Longarm deferred to Billy and let the marshal lead out at a swift jog.

They reached their ambush point without raising either sweat or dust and well ahead of the riders. If, that is, the riders were still moving toward them. They were too close now and too low to see. They had to take it on blind faith that the riders had not altered their line of travel.

By unspoken consent both men remained on their horses. A solid, dismounted rest was better for shooting, but staying in the saddle would make it possible to give chase more quickly.

Billy stopped at the fringe of the plum thicket. Longarm rode across the flat to the other side of the swale—the coulee the riders were following had broadened and become shallow at this end—and stopped in the shade of an ancient, dying cottonwood. Billy was ninety or a hundred yards in front of him. If the gang wanted to put up a scrap, the two of them would have the robbers caught in a crossfire.

They waited the expected ten minutes. Then fifteen. Then twenty. Either the riders had slowed their pace or changed direction. Longarm's horse pushed at the bit, trying to drop its muzzle toward the few tufts of drying, brittle grass that were able to survive in the shade of the old tree. He brought its head up again.

Thirty minutes now, he judged. The horse was becoming impatient, but a glance across the swale toward the plum thicket showed that Billy was not. The marshal looked like he could wait there through the snows of winter without becoming nervous if he had to. And the play was Billy's. It would be up to him to decide if he wanted to sit it out where they were or ride for a better look.

Billy sat on his horse and yawned. Longarm smiled a little. This was a game Billy Vail had played many and many a time before. A little dose of the unexpected wasn't going to spook him into doing anything he didn't want to.

Thirty-five minutes. Longarm could hear hoofbeats now. A good many of them and moving slowly. Horses that had been run hard all the way from Broomfield would be flagging now. No wonder the riders had slowed before they got this far. At least there would be no long chase. Tired as those horses had to be, they would be no match for Billy's and Longarm's, even if they were top-quality stock trying to outrun livery mounts. Not after this much of a run across country.

Soon Longarm could hear the labored breathing of the horses. One animal snorted and blew, and Longarm heard its rider mutter. The sound of bit chains and creaking saddle leather carried clear on the thin air.

Across the way Billy Vail palmed his Colt and gathered his reins ready to move out and make the challenge.

A rider came into view and then another.

Billy nudged his horse out of the plums.

"U.S. marshals. Stand where you are." He played no amateur game of flashing a badge with one hand and a gun in the other. He needed his reins and his gun and the hell with the badge.

The riders' attention focused on Vail, and Longarm moved his horse into position behind them.

There was something wrong, though. There weren't five riders who had been making all that dust, there were—he counted quickly—eleven of them. They looked tired and sweaty and pissed off, and most of them were dressed for city streets in narrow-brimmed hats and ties and sleeve garters.

"Hold your fire," a man in the lead said quickly. "We're a posse out o' Broomfield. You say you're marshals?"

"Damn," Billy answered.

"If this is what I think it is, then I agree with you," the Broomfield police chief said.

Billy moved forward to show his badge and verify that the riders were who they said they were. Only when he had done that did he give Longarm a nod.

Longarm relaxed his vigilance and pushed his Colt back into its holster.

He gave the Broomfield posse quite a start when they realized they had been covered from behind all this time. They hadn't seen him there until Billy motioned him forward.

Which was no satisfaction at all under the circumstances.

Longarm and Billy had gone and trapped themselves the wrong bunch.

Chapter 21

"There wasn't anybody running ahead of you," Vail assured the Broomfield possemen. "We were in position well ahead of you and saw your dust, but there wasn't anything in front of you."

"Damn," someone said. The Broomfield men dismounted and loosened their cinches. Their horses were damn well worn out by the run they had made, and some of them would need considerable recuperation before they could be turned around for the long ride back.

The man leading the posse was Police Chief Aaron Mason. He had one officer with him. The rest were townspeople who had grabbed horses and guns on the spur of the moment. None of them had come away prepared for a long chase, and most of them looked like they were grateful that it was over with now.

"Would you mind telling us what happened?" Billy asked. "It's our jurisdiction, of course, but all we know is that your post office was hit."

"I'd damn well say it was hit," Mason said bitterly. "I'm short on details myself, y'understand. Thought it was more important to get after the sons o' bitches than stand around making notes. But the way I hear it, they hit, oh, a couple hours ago, I guess it was. Something like that. I've kinda lost track o' the time since. Come in in broad daylight an' bold as brass. Three inside an' two out front holdin' horses for 'em." Mason pulled a plug of tobacco out of his pocket and bit off a piece of it.

"There was some customers inside. Four, five people. An', of course, Bernie Kreiter an' Jim Jeckman behind the counter. Bernie is our postmaster and Jim's his clerk. Or was." He made a face.

"Was?"

"Yes, damnit, was. Mind you, we'd all heard about the robberies down to Englewood an' Aurora. Bernie and me talked about that over coffee just this morning. He was worried. Not so much for himself but what could happen to folks if there was a bunch of crazy assholes with guns. I expect he was right t' worry too." He shook his head.

"Anyhow, these bastards come inside with masks—"

"Sacks over their heads," one of the possemen said. "I saw them. They were sacks with cutouts for their eyes. Flour sacks. Tater sacks. Something like that."

Mason nodded. "Yeah. Anyway, these three come inside quick and mean. Had their guns out an' knew what they wanted. One of 'em held a gun on the customers while the other two went behind the counter. Bernie, he put his hands up an' called out real loud for everybody else to stay calm an' do the same. Said it wasn't worth anybody getting killed for the few dollars he had in the drawer. He . . . afterward, see . . . Bernie kept saying about that over an' over. Saying how he'd told everybody t' be calm an' nothing would happen. Saying how it wasn't worth a killing for a few dollars." He shook his head again.

"Anyway, they're all in there, the robbers with their guns and everybody else with their hands up an' then I guess something happened, I don't know what, and—"

"Aaron," one of the possemen put in.

"Yeah?"

"While you were with Bernie I heard that part of it from Tim Fulbright."

"What was it?" the Broomfield police chief asked.

"It was Laurie Ridder," the posseman said. "You know how Jeckman was sweet on her."

Mason nodded.

"Well, Laurie was one of the folks in the place at the

time. She was in line at the counter there. And when the robbers had the customers up against the wall with their hands up, this one sonuvabitch that was covering them walks over and takes hold of Laurie's . . . well . . . you know. He takes hold of the front of Laurie and squeezes. And, of course, Laurie"— he looked at Vail and Longarm and shrugged— "Laurie is a shy girl. Real pretty but real shy. And real religious. She teaches Sunday school and all that, and I doubt she's ever kissed a fella much less done anything that she oughtn't. We all know what she's like and respect her for it, Jim Jeckman included. So I expect it was kind of shocking that somebody would go and do a thing like that to Laurie. So when this guy *did*, well, Jim put his hands down and started for him. Of course there was the counter between them, and Jim wasn't armed anyway. But the leader of the bunch, big son of a bitch, Fulbright said . . . he was one of the other folks in the post office, you see, so he'd know . . . this leader of the bunch turns and points his gun at Jim . . . they were only a few feet apart . . . and shoots him right in the side of the head. I mean, Jim was only worried about Laurie and wanted to help her. But this son of a bitch shot Jim down in cold blood, right in front of Laurie. Shot him right in the head."

"Jesus," Mason said.

Several of the possemen, who obviously hadn't heard that part of it themselves, looked off toward the mountains with dark glares even though the gang hadn't gone in that direction. It was the way they'd been chasing the robbers, so it was still the direction the posse members thought of in their anger.

"Poor Laurie," someone said.

"Poor Laurie, hell. Poor Jim," another put in.

"Bastard," someone else said.

"This man who shot the clerk," Longarm asked. "You say he was a big man? Did anyone get a good look at him?"

"I saw him when he was coming out of the post office," a thin, bespectacled man without a hat said. "I heard the shot and walked out onto the sidewalk to see what it was about. I saw the horses and the people at the post office, and I saw the three men come outside. There was a lot of shouting inside quick as they cleared the door, but of course, nobody in there was armed. But I saw the robbers."

"Could you describe the big one for me?"

"Sure. About as big a man as I've seen in a long time. Huge, lumpy shoulders on him. Sack over his head and a tall hat with four pinches in the crown, whatever you call that. Gun belt. Tall boots. Let me see now." The man closed his eyes and tried to remember. "Plaid shirt. Blue, I think it was. Blue and black and white plaid but mostly blue. Black broadcloth trousers. The shirt and trousers looked new. The hat didn't." Longarm was willing to bet that the man sold clothes in a Broomfield store. "Great big man, anyway. Huge." He snapped his fingers. "Oh, yes. He limped when he walked, and he got on his horse from the right side. I remember that clear now."

It was Big again. No doubting that, of course. Not that there really was any doubt to begin with, but . . . Longarm gave Billy a look of silent apology. The pressures were going to grow faster than ever with another federal employee dead. And the fault lying square on Longarm's doorstep.

"Anyway," Mason picked up, "they cleaned the place out and got on their horses. They knew right where they were going. They took off at a run. I'd heard the shots and was already on my way. As soon as I heard what happened, I called for volunteers, and we started after them. They had a good ten or fifteen minutes lead by the time we could all grab horses and guns and get after them. We sure as hell thought they were headed for the mountains. That's the way they were pointed the last anyone saw them. But . . ." He shrugged. "Here you

110

have it. You say they weren't running in front of us when you picked up our dust."

"We were keeping watch a good half hour before we spotted your dust, and we could see for miles in front of you from where we were," Billy told him. "They pulled off somewhere that you didn't see. I'm positive they weren't running in front of you."

"Son of a bitch," someone complained.

"I sure do want those bastards," Mason said.

"Not a bit more than we do," Billy Vail told him.

Longarm scowled. There wasn't a one of them who wanted this gang more than he did.

And Big Little most of all.

Chapter 22

Longarm brooded on the way back to Denver.

Big and his gang had hit post offices now in Englewood, Aurora and Broomfield. All of them close to
Denver but all of them in towns small enough, and out
far enough, that the gang members had little to fear
about either opposition or escape.

The robberies had been brutal but almost laughably
easy.

The robbers hit, took what they wanted and rode
quickly away. In none of the robberies had a posse been
able to find the gang afterward.

They had gotten away easily. To the mountains near
the Bar Horseshoe Bar? Possibly before. The presence
of a rifleman waiting along the trail near there indicated
it was a good likelihood. Yet the bunch that hit Broomfield had *not* run for the foothills. Longarm and Billy
were ahead of them this time. They would have seen if
the five riders were running in front of the posse. Somewhere, somehow, the raiders had veered away from the
expected path and made off in an as yet unknown direction.

Longarm frowned and shifted lower on the uphol-
stery of the passenger car.

He wanted a smoke, but the last time he pulled out a
cheroot a woman traveling with two bratty children
asked him—and none too politely either—to refrain.
Her little darlings were asthmatic, and cigar smoke
bothered them.

Longarm grunted and gave the woman a sideways
glance of disapproval. She didn't want his smoke to

bother them, but it seemed perfectly all right if the little monsters bothered everyone else in the car with their whining and wheedling.

Their mother was oblivious to the discomforts of others, though. She made no attempt to silence her snotty brats and was sitting there seemingly content.

"I'm going out on the platform," Longarm said abruptly.

Billy nodded and stayed where he was. The marshal had been quiet for most of the journey, his thoughts contained but his expression no brighter than Longarm's.

They were already rolling through the outskirts of Denver when Longarm leaned against the platform railing and carefully nipped the twisted tip off a cheroot. He cupped his hands against the breeze of the train's movement and struck a match. The smoke drawn deep into his lungs tasted good. When he exhaled it was whipped away on the wind.

Little and his men had to be somewhere near, damn them.

But where?

Not in the hills above the Sawyer place. Not now, or Billy and Longarm would have been in position to intercept them. Whether they had been camped there before or not was still an open question, but now Longarm had little expectation that the Boulder posse would find anything. An empty camp with cold fires at the best.

Longarm continued to stand at the railing, smoking and fretting, until the short-haul train jolted and shuddered to a stop at the Denver depot. Longarm hopped down to the platform and waited for Billy to join him. The marshal had left his horse in Broomfield. A man at the livery there was supposed to return the animal to its owner in Boulder. Longarm's gear and rented horse were in a car near the tail of the train.

"I'll see you in the morning," Billy told him.

Longarm shook his head. "I'm not going back to my

room tonight, Billy. I'm going on down to Englewood, I think."

Vail raised an eyebrow.

"I'm missing something. There has to be some damn thing to point me toward Little. Whatever it is, I've been missing it. I won't find it here, though. I'm going to look around Englewood some more, then maybe go out to the Circle Y and talk to Pat Vieren again."

"All right."

"If anything turns up, send me a wire care of the Englewood police. I'll check with them before I head off in any new directions."

"All right."

The woman with the snotty kids brushed past on the platform, carrying one and dragging the older of them squalling and yammering by a wet hand. Longarm did not envy that one's husband.

Vail started toward the hansom stand, and Longarm turned back toward the livestock car.

"Billy," he called when they were a few yards apart.

"Yes?"

"Try not to assault any more public officials while I'm away, will you? It's embarrassing to the rest of us." Longarm grinned.

Billy Vail made a rude gesture in his direction and trudged off. If Longarm knew him, though, the marshal would not be taking a cab toward the comforts of home tonight. Billy would likely spend most of the evening at his desk again.

It was going to be a hell of a loss to the entire district—no, to the entire Justice Department—if Billy Vail was jerked out of that office.

And if that happened, Custis Long was the person who would be responsible for it.

The thought gave Longarm no comfort at all as he continued down the line of cars to claim his horse.

Chapter 23

It was nearly nine o'clock when Longarm reached Englewood, much too late to find Joe Doyle or the Englewood police chief still at work. Longarm left a message for Doyle telling the sergeant where he could be reached, then looked for a store keeping late hours.

There was no place open where he could buy any groceries, so he settled for making a café man's evening and ordered a large basket of fried chicken, two pies left over from the dinner trade and several loaves of bread that would be stale if left overnight.

"Funny time to be going on a picnic, mister," the man at the café observed.

"Everybody's entitled to a quirk or two," Longarm said, rather than offering an explanation. He tied the hamper of food behind his saddle and rode to Sally Anne Hufnagel's tiny house.

She was asleep when he got there. It took her several minutes to answer his knock. When she opened the door she was sleepy eyed, and her hair was in tangles. She smiled when she saw who the caller was, though, and her kiss was warm and welcoming.

Her nightshift was thin and much patched, but in the pale illumination of the moonlight she looked tempting. And her body pressing eagerly against his was even more so.

"I brought some supper."

"You didn't have to do that."

"I know."

She pulled him inside and latched the door closed,

115

then made it entirely clear that she was more interested in the messenger than the message. Supper could wait.

Longarm hadn't eaten since dinner at the Bar Horseshoe Bar, but he agreed with Sally Anne. Supper could wait.

He pulled her to him and felt the urgency in her slim body as she rocked her pelvis against his. He picked her up and carried her to the well-remembered bed.

The shift slid off her shoulders almost of its own volition. There was no light in the little room save a faint, red glow from the stove. He ran his hands over her body, and she moaned softly and raised herself to him. Her fingers fumbled awkwardly at his buttons.

"Want me to do that for you, ma'am?" he asked in a slow, laconic drawl.

"Yes. Please. Quickly."

Sally Anne kissed him and tried to help while he shed his clothes and joined her on the narrow bed. Her skin was cool to the touch but heated rapidly. Her body was light and lithe and quickly moist.

He touched her, in no hurry at all now, and she groaned and wrapped her arms tight around him as Longarm poised over her and then lowered himself onto and into her.

Her warm, receptive flesh enveloped his, and she strained upward to meet him.

"I was having the nicest dream when you came. It was about you. But this is nicer." She kissed his chest and rocked her hips gently up and down.

Longarm held himself rigid over her and allowed Sally Anne to skewer herself on him at a slow, comfortable pace.

As her breathing quickened so did her hips. She scissored her legs around his waist and locked her ankles together behind him, grasping now and slapping her flat belly against his.

"Oh, my. This is . . . this is . . ." She cried out and shuddered, convulsing tight around him.

"Damn," she muttered.

"What's wrong?"

"It's over, that's what's wrong," she complained.

Longarm smiled at her. "Actually," he said, "we're a long way from it being over." He shrugged. "Unless you want to quit, that is." Teasingly he began to withdraw from her.

"No," she cried quickly. She clung to him all the tighter and brought him deep inside her once again.

"If you're sure," he said.

She laughed and covered his neck with quick, fluttering kisses. "I'm sure."

He began to move inside her.

"Pretty sure," she amended.

He stopped.

Sally Anne laughed and bit him on the shoulder.

"Ouch."

"Do your duty, Deputy, or it's more of the same."

"I expect I'm at your mercy, then."

"And don't you forget it, either." She laughed again and snuggled happily against him as he resumed the gentle, pleasant motion.

This second time too Longarm hung back, controlling himself until he felt the gathering rise of Sally Anne's pleasure in her breathing and her responses, in the small, involuntary contractions and pumpings of her slender body beneath him.

Only then did he surrender control and allow himself to plunge and plunder, taking satisfaction from her and giving more back to her.

It was quite a while before they got around to thinking about a late supper. Longarm didn't think Sally Anne minded that any more than he did.

"Something is bothering you."

Longarm looked at her. His expression had been impassive, he was sure. People who had known him a very

117

long time were not usually perceptive enough to read him that well. He set his fork down and shrugged.

"Do you want to tell me about it?" she offered.

"No." He smiled and leaned over to kiss her. Then, most unusual for him, he began to tell her about it anyway. The little laundress from Englewood was remarkably easy to talk to, and he discovered with a sense of mild amazement that he wanted to talk.

She frowned when he was done and moved her chair closer so she could hold his hand and lay her head on his shoulder. "It is all so complicated, isn't it. I feel simply horrid for Chester. I'm sorry, dear. I can't help it. I do. But I think you are a good man too. I don't want you to lose your job. Or your Mr. Vail. The way you talk about him" —she smiled—"he must be almost as fine a man as you."

"That's the really bad part of this whole thing," Longarm said. "I mean, I can get along. I'm willing to pay for my own mistakes. The thing that really bothers me is that now it looks like Billy might have to pay for my mistakes too. He's a good man, Sally Anne. And I don't mean just at his job. He is a genuinely good man."

"So are you, dear."

"Not so damn good, though, that I don't let a murderer go free to murder again. That poor fellow in Broomfield died today because I didn't do my job when I had the chance to put Big in cuffs. I should have . . ." He didn't finish the sentence. But then, he didn't have to.

Sally Anne pressed closer against him, as if her presence, the warmth from her body and the genuine concern expressed in her touch, could somehow make it better.

"If there was anything I could do . . ." she said. "Anything. I would do it, dear. I promise you I would."

"I know." He forced a smile. "I know you would, and I appreciate you wanting to." He bent and kissed her forehead lightly.

"I really tried to think, after you left, that is, if there was anything I'd forgotten to tell you while you were here before. Anything Chester might have mentioned to me that could help. Now I wish all the more that I'd been able to think of something. But I couldn't. Not really. Certainly nothing important."

"Something unimportant then?" he asked. The thing was, you just never really knew what was important.

Sally Anne shrugged. "The only thing I could remember that I haven't told you already was about his sister."

"Big has a sister? Somewhere around here?" He could feel a surge of quick excitement. If Big had kin close by . . .

"No," Sally Anne said, bringing his hopes crashing down as quickly as they had risen. "That's what I mean. It couldn't possibly be important. Chester does have a sister, but she lives in Nebraska. Eastern Nebraska, at that." Her forehead wrinkled in concentration. "Fremont? That might've been it. Is there a Fremont in Nebraska?"

"Yeah," Longarm acknowledged. "Not too far from Omaha, if I remember right." He sighed. "Too damn far away for anybody to ride out and knock over a post office in Broomfield, that's for sure."

"I'm sorry," Sally Anne said. "I truly want to help you, but I simply haven't been able to think of anything else Chester said. If he wasn't at that place with the buckskin horses . . ."

Longarm finished the last of the coffee Sally Anne had made for him, using beans he had brought her before.

With a deliberate effort of will he dragged his thoughts off his troubles and placed them on this gentle girl beside him who was so eager to please. And to be pleased. He hugged her and fondled one tender, quickly hard nipple.

Sally Anne's breathing quickened almost at once, and she seemed to melt to his touch.

"You, uh, wouldn't mind going back to bed now?" he asked.

"If you don't take me there this instant, Custis Long, I shall drag you to it kicking and screaming. I swear I will."

He smiled. "Wouldn't want to put you to all that trouble, ma'am." He picked her up, feather light in his arms, and carried her away from the table.

Chapter 24

Sergeant Joe Doyle shook his head. "No, no messages for you, Longarm." He hid a yawn behind his hand and stretched. "Look, I haven't had breakfast yet. Want to join me?"

"Sure. I haven't eaten yet, either." Longarm hadn't wanted to take anything out of Sally Anne's meager larder, so he had pretended lack of hunger earlier. He followed Doyle to a café two blocks from the police station and ordered a heap of everything they had. Or close to it, anyway.

"Almost forgot," Doyle said. He reached inside his coat and pulled out a folded sheet of paper. "When you were here before you asked Al Tyrel to make you out a list of everything that was taken?"

Longarm had to think back for a moment, then he remembered and nodded. "I expect I did, but I forgot about it until you mentioned it just now."

Doyle pushed the paper across the table. "He gave it to me yesterday and wanted me to pass it along to you when I saw you next. I, uh, sat down and made myself a copy of it. Hope you don't mind."

"Of course not."

Longarm examined the list while he was waiting for his breakfast to be delivered. There was nothing particularly surprising on it.

Cash and stamps valued at $814.21. Approximately.

Thirty-two blank postal money orders, which if filled out and cashed at other post offices could be worth damn near whatever the bearer wanted.

Assorted pins and pens and gum bands worth something less than a dollar. The dead postmaster's clerk, Albert Tyrel, had scrupulously listed each item he thought he remembered, no matter how trivial.

Beneath the list of post office materials, Tyrel had drawn a line and added on the same sheet a separate list showing things his customers recalled putting in the outgoing mail that morning.

There was little cash involved. Two customers had sent cash to mail-order business houses, their orders totaling something under $15. One sent a money order in the amount of $38 made out to a wholesale supply house in Saint Louis. A woman had mailed two dollar bills to her sister in Taos. Everything else on the list was correspondence, although Tyrel noted at the bottom of the sheet that several businessmen in the community were extremely upset to think that their business correspondence might have fallen into unknown hands.

The postal clerk and former cavalryman had done a thorough job filling Longarm's request for information. Beside each item shown was the name of the person who had mailed the cash or money order or letter or whatever.

Longarm just wished to hell he had some positive use he could put Tyrel's lists toward. He refolded the sheet and slipped it into his coat pocket.

The waiter returned with a heavily laden tray and deposited most of the food in front of Longarm. The owner of the café Doyle had brought Longarm to gave full value for the customer's money. A simple order of fried potatoes didn't cover part of Longarm's plate; it occupied an entire serving bowl all its own. And that was only one of the dishes Longarm had asked for.

Doyle saw the look on Longarm's face when all of it was piled in front of him. The Englewood sergeant chuckled. "Eat hearty, friend."

Chapter 25

The big man with the belly and the fancy vest that was barely able to cover it ignored Longarm and glared at Joe Doyle.

He stalked inside the restaurant with a frown, jerked out the chair that sat empty between Doyle's and Longarm's and turned it so he sat almost face-on to the Englewood sergeant and his back half turned to the federal deputy.

"Well?" he demanded. He jammed a thick cigar between his teeth and leaned forward on one elbow so that he was nearly nose-to-nose with Doyle.

Doyle refused to be intimidated. He gave the newcomer a tight, thin smile and said, "Good morning."

"Fuck that," the fleshy, flashy man said. "Have you accomplished anything?" He snorted. "Why do I bother to ask. Of course you haven't. You couldn't find your ass if you happened to be sitting on it."

Doyle's expression did not change. But then Longarm held no delusions that he had meant the smile to begin with. "Mr. Creel, the gentleman behind you there is Deputy Marshal Custis Long. Marshal Long"—he motioned—"Marvin Creel." He let it go at that and reached for his coffee cup. Doyle was nearly finished with his breakfast. Longarm had gotten around just about all he could of his own.

Creel swiveled in his chair to face Longarm with a frown no more welcoming or pleasant than the one he had given Doyle. He grunted loudly. "Long, eh? Read about you. Another fucking incompetent." He turned back to Doyle as if Longarm was not worth considering any further.

"Nice fella," Longarm said to Joe, his voice mild.

"Salt of the earth," Joe agreed.

"Are you two assholes done making jokes?" Creel demanded. "Why don't you both quit sitting here drawing pay and go out and find the son of a bitch who murdered Mack Bowen." He took the cigar out of his face and waved it under Doyle's chin. Some ash dribbled onto Joe's plate. Creel obviously saw but made no apology. Joe Doyle calmly laid his knife and fork down and pushed the plate away.

"I want you to know, Doyle. You make good on this arrest and you do it damned quick, or I'll have your badge in my pocket." Creel reached over and, deliberately this time, tapped his cigar ash onto what was left of Joe Doyle's eggs.

Apparently Billy Vail was not the only peace officer in the Denver area who was in deep political shit over the current spate of post office robberies, Longarm saw.

Doyle took the threat calmly enough. His smile faded and was replaced with a cold, hard look that would have made most men back off. "Are you done, Marvin?"

"Not by half. But *you* are, mister. Believe it." Creel stuck the cigar back into his jaw, gave Doyle another grade-A glare and stomped away without a second glance at Longarm.

Longarm watched the man sail out of the crowded café and then looked at Doyle and lifted an eyebrow. "Mind if I ask what that was all about?"

Now that Creel was gone, Longarm could see how troubled Doyle was by the quick, nasty little visit. He had hidden it well while Creel was in sight, but it damn sure bothered him. The fact that everyone else in the place had overheard only made it all that much worse. Joe dropped his eyes and shrugged.

Later, though, when they were outside on the street, Doyle explained.

"That cocksucker Creel was putting on an act," he said. "He wants to make sure everybody knows how deeply distressed he is about Mr. Bowen being dead and how much he wants the killers found."

"Oh?" Nothing more. Longarm suspected Doyle needed an outlet right now, not actual questions. The sergeant needed a chance to talk, preferably with someone who was not involved in the local political scene. Longarm waited and gave him time to get it out.

"You don't know Creel?"

Longarm shook his head.

"You'll hear about him soon enough now that Mr. Bowen is gone. Mr. Bowen, he was a politician through and through, but he wasn't all that bad a sort, if you know what I mean."

Longarm did. There were bad politicians and there were some not so bad.

"Marvin Creel is a blustering, bragging, butt-brain. Which is probably a huge surprise to you." He smiled. "When Mr. Bowen was alive, Marvin was his big competition for being in charge of things around here. Patronage, jobs, work contracts, like that. Mr. Bowen ran it, mostly. Creel wanted to. They couldn't stand each other. Now that Mack is dead, Creel is already taking over. And any tears he sheds about Mack being dead are damn sure of the crocodile kind. He's glad as hell, though o' course he can't admit it out loud. The SOB meant what he said about my badge, too, of course. He'll have it anyway, sooner or later. He only wants an excuse to take it. Which is what that bullshit in the restaurant was all about. He wants everyone to know that he isn't putting me on the outs because he wants to but because I haven't found Mack's killer. O' course I already know who he'll put in to replace me. The oldest son of one of his cronies is a kiss-ass office deputy with the sheriff here. Creel wants to cement the relationship with the crony by putting the kid in a safe, good-paying spot on the city payroll." He shrugged. "And since the kid is interested in flashing a badge for all the girlies to see, Creel has decided my job is the one he wants for his buddy's son."

"I see." Longarm pulled out a pair of cheroots and offered one to Doyle. Both men lit up and stood in the shade of a porch overhang.

"Creel is part of a new wave in politics around here. Tied in somehow with a crowd of power-hungry boys in Denver with a guy named Parkhurst. I don't know him. Maybe you do."

"Leonidas B. Parkhurst. Sure, I know him." It was the asshole Billy Vail had had the fuss with—and thrown out of the office.

"I mean, I've heard of this Parkhurst before, but he runs more in your neighborhood than in mine, so I can't say that I really know him. Anyway, Creel is wanting to be the top dog around here, just like Parkhurst intends to be the bull o' the woods around the place with the gold dome." The gold dome Doyle referred to was the Capitol Building at the corner of Colfax and Broadway. "I hear both of them intend to do some serious house cleaning once they have things in order."

Longarm grunted. "So I understand. Your badge, my badge, Marshal Vail's badge, too, for that matter."

"Even Marshal Vail's?"

Longarm nodded.

"That would be a shame. He's a good man the way I hear it."

"So he is."

"So was Mr. Bowen, in his way. I mean, there were a lot of little things a guy could bitch about if he really wanted to. But Mr. Bowen never let any of the graft be the kind that could hurt anybody. A guy might suck at the public trough and draw pay that he never earned. But it was only a little payoff money. You know? Never anything that really counted. He never messed with the police force here, for instance. Never once told us there was anybody we couldn't put in the slam or any place

126

we couldn't hit if we needed to. That was always clear. Even things like the tax collector's job. There wasn't anything going into anybody's pockets except salary. We had a clerk try to embezzle some extra one time, and we put the guy away for two to five. Mr. Bowen told us we'd done a good job, even though the clerk was a brother-in-law of one of Mack's friends."

"Sounds like you got along all right with Bowen," Longarm observed.

"We did. Nothing's perfect, o' course. But Mr. Bowen knew where to draw the lines. He kept things running all right." Doyle glanced down the street in the direction Creel had gone. "With that fish-breath son of a bitch in charge I'm afraid it will be different. An' not for the better."

"Same deal in Denver if Parkhurst sneaks into a power position. Except then the whole damned state will be for sale," Longarm agreed.

"Heaven protect us from politicians," Doyle said.

Longarm finished his cheroot and crushed the butt out under the sole of his boot. "That's what it will take to protect us from that kind." He grinned. "And since that happens to be out of my jurisdiction, I expect I'd best head out to the Circle Y and try again to get a line on Big. Wish me luck, Joe. Maybe I can save your job while I'm at it."

Doyle laughed, some bitterness intruding in the tone of it. "No chance if Creel gets in. But maybe you can help keep some poor bastard alive by breaking the gang before they lift your tin. I'll wish you luck on that account."

"Luck to both of us," Longarm said. He waved good-bye to the Englewood sergeant and walked toward his horse.

Chapter 26

A man can't pan the same tiny patch of gravel but so many times before he has to expect to run out of color. But damnit, Longarm had nothing else to go on. No place new to turn. The Circle Y was where they knew Big the best, so that was where he had to keep turning in his efforts to find something, anything, that would give him a handle on where Big might be now.

It was midmorning when he rode into the ranch yard again. As usual there was a curl of smoke rising from the house chimney. As usual Longarm bypassed the house in favor of the barn area to look for Tom Lee and Pat Vieren. He found Pat beyond the barns, busy forking hay into a bunker at the near end of the mare pasture. The day was not particularly warm, but Vieren was working with furious energy and was running sweat. He seemed to be attacking the hay with the tines of the pitchfork.

"Good morning," Longarm said from the saddle.

Vieren turned with a quick scowl that was as quickly moderated when he saw who the visitor was. "Oh, it's you, Longarm. Step down." He managed a smile then.

"Are you all right, Pat?"

"Just pissed off."

Longarm dismounted and tied the horse to a nearby post.

Vieren shoved the pitchfork into the haystack, stripped off his gloves and wiped the sweat from his forehead. "Sorry. I thought for a minute there you were another of those damned bounty hunters. The sons of bitches have been lurking around the place like a bunch

128

of damned vultures. They're making Althea nervous."
He made a face. "Then to top it all off, I'm having to do
everything myself now."

"I guess I don't understand." Longarm pulled out
two cheroots, gave one to Vieren and struck a match to
light both smokes. "Lee quit you or something?" Longarm had talked to the man right here just yesterday
morning.

"Didn't quit. I had to fire him. Sure didn't want to
with Big gone, but Tom got sassy with me yesterday. I
asked him to clean out a stall and he told me he'd get
around to it after dinner. Can you imagine that? Told me
he'd do it when he got around to it. Had no choice but
to fire him, of course. Which he knew good as I did. A
man can't put up with that sorta thing. What I think is
that he wanted to leave but decided he'd rather be fired
than quit. So now I'm stuck with doing all the work
when I really need two hands to help me with all that
needs done." Vieren frowned.

"I see what you mean," Longarm said sympathetically.

Vieren shrugged. "Anyway, what with no help and
the damn bounty hunters all over the place, I expect I'm
just not in a very good humor today. Sorry." He sighed,
then smiled again. "Now that I've got my bellyaching
out of the way, Longarm, what can I do for you?"

"Same old deal," Longarm admitted. "Still looking
for help."

"I don't know, Longarm. I still can't believe Big
pulled one robbery, much less two."

"Three," Longarm corrected.

"Three?"

Longarm told him about the Broomfield holdup and
murder.

Vieren whistled and shook his head. "Damn."

"Yeah. Damn indeed. But it was Big and his pals
again, Pat. I'm sorry, but there's just no getting around

it. Same story as before. It was definitely Big that led them and did the shooting."

Vieren shook his head again. He seemed sadder than ever after Longarm's unwelcome news.

"I really need your help, Pat."

"I've already told you—"

"I know. I know that, Pat, and I appreciate it. Truly I do. But what I need . . . look, I understand Big has a sister in Nebraska. But how 'bout around here? Do you know of any kin he has close?"

"Nobody," Vieren said. "Hell, Longarm, I didn't even know about the sister. He never mentioned kinfolk that I recall."

"What about friends, then? There are five other guys in on these robberies. Can you give me any help about who one of them might be?"

Vieren frowned and pulled on the cheroot Longarm had lit for him. He thought it over for a moment before he spoke. "It's kinda funny now that I think on it. But I can't bring to mind one single man that I'd say was an extra close friend to Big. I mean, hell, everybody was Big's friend. I don't expect the man ever met anybody that *wasn't* his friend. If you know what I mean. But nobody in *particular*, you see. No real close pals. Nobody that he really partnered with. I mean, the guy was buddies with whoever was near. But nobody ever come by here to visit with him, and I don't guess I ever heard him mention anybody that he was going to see special. Though the past month or so he'd go off in the evenings more often than he used to, and he'd get kinda spiffed up before he left. But he never said where he was going or who he expected to see."

Longarm grunted. That information was no help. Longarm already knew where Big had been going and what the big man had been doing of late. He'd been going in to Englewood to see Sally Anne Hufnagel and take his reading lessons from her. Damnit.

And Sally Anne swore that he never mentioned any particular close friends to her either.

"Nobody from the outfits he used to work with down south? Nothing like that?"

Vieren shook his head again. "None that I can recall." He sounded sincere about it. Longarm did not have the impression that Pat Vieren was trying to hide anything from him. "It's kind of odd, isn't it, that a man so friendly and popular wouldn't really have any close pals. I guess I just never thought about it before now."

Or not so odd, Longarm realized. Big Little was a big, happy, friendly fellow. But he wasn't sharp enough to talk with much. Big freely said as much about himself. Had done so, in fact, the last time Longarm talked with him, right here at the Circle Y. He just wasn't the sort of person a man would seek out for companionship. Everybody liked Big. But nobody sought him out or buddied up with him, particularly. Custis Long included.

So who the hell were these five other guys in the gang?

Longarm had been paying so much attention to the *one* identifiable member of the post office robbery crowd that he'd as good as forgotten that there were *six* men in the bunch.

He gnawed on the soggy tip of his cheroot and frowned.

There was something . . . he couldn't quite nail the thought down, but there were half-formed notions flickering somewhere down deep in his mind, notions that said there was something to that that should be pulled out and examined once the ideas got themselves together enough to be presentable for inspection.

Later, he decided. He would let the notion germinate and come out to the fore in its own good time. Whatever it was.

Longarm grunted and thanked Pat Vieren once again for trying to help.

"You could do me a favor in return," Vieren suggested.

"If I can."

"It's about these damned bounty hunters." He pointed, and Longarm could see a pair of horsemen sitting in the shade of a distant stand of willow. He'd noticed them before but assumed they were a pair of locals innocently loafing in the shade. Their horses were beside the right-of-way along the public road to Denver. "They're really making Althea nervous, Longarm. Could you do something about sending them packing?"

"I can talk to them, Pat, but I have to tell you that I don't think it will do much good. Unless they're trespassing on private property or breaking some other law, there isn't much I can do to help. They have a right to sit and watch."

Vieren sighed. "That's what the county deputy said too."

"I'll talk to them," Longarm promised.

"Thanks."

"But tell your wife not to get her hopes up. They might be there until this thing is over with, one way or another."

"I know we aren't really in any danger from them. Althea does too. But we're both of us scared something could happen if Big decides to come back here for some reason. And we think he might. You know?"

"Sure. So do they. That's why they're waiting where they can keep an eye on the house." Longarm shrugged. "I'll talk to them, Pat."

Longarm dropped the butt of his cigar into the dirt and ground it underfoot, then turned toward his horse. "If you hear anything . . ."

There was no point in finishing it. If Big Little showed up here to talk to Pat and Althea Vieren, the

132

bounty hunters would know about it long before any lawman did.

"See you later, Longarm."

He mounted and rode up the lane toward the Denver road.

Chapter 27

The two "men" didn't look much like Longarm's idea of what a bounty hunter should be.

At least in theory a bounty hunter should be tough, competent and handy with a gun. A man pretty much had to have those qualities, at least to some degree, if he expected to survive the process of trying to make a buck by bringing other, often desperate, men to justice.

These boys looked broke, bored and much too young to be going around issuing challenges to their betters. And if Longarm's judgment was valid after getting a good look at them, damn near any man was their better.

Neither of them was old enough to shave, much less to vote, and their belly guns looked like the sort of thing you could pick out of a gunsmith's parts barrel for fifty cents. If the gunsmith was a greedy man. One had a rusty old war-years Smith & Wesson rimfire stuffed behind his belt. The other carried a battered and abused thing in his pants pocket. Longarm wasn't sure—he could only see the cracked grips—but he thought the pipsqueak little thing was an Ivor Johnson .22. Incredible.

He hid his amusement and touched the brim of his hat in greeting when he reined the horse to a stop in front of them.

"Gentlemen." He seriously doubted either one of them was able to discern the irony in his voice.

"We're here first, mister," one of them answered nervously. "We got first dibs on the murderer."

First dibs? Lordy! The boy looked like he *might* have hit his sixteenth birthday. And Althea Vieren was wor-

134

ried about these kids? Both of them looked like they ought to be still raiding watermelon patches, not hunting men.

The one who had spoken wore threadbare jeans and boots that looked to be older than he was. The other one was a year or two his senior. He affected leather wrist cuffs and had a pair of gloves tucked behind his belt— he was the one who carried his revolver in his pocket, probably so it wouldn't get in the way of the gloves— that were supposed to make him look like a top hand.

Longarm introduced himself to the youngsters and showed his badge. "You're here waiting for the post office murderers, I take it?"

"Yes, sir."

Longarm grunted and hooked a knee over the pommel of his old McClellan. Both of the boys, he noticed, rode decent horseflesh and clean, well-maintained stock saddles.

"Been trailing cows, have you?"

"Yes, sir."

"Outfit broke up last week," the other boy volunteered. "Damned owner went bust."

"That's what he told us, anyhow."

"Said the beeves was being repossessed and there wasn't any money to pay us."

"We got hung out t' dry, Marshal."

"We got to do something so's we can get home."

"We got to find that Mr. Little, Marshal. We *got* to."

Longarm nodded sympathetically. "You do know, I suppose, that you're making Mrs. Vieren nervous, you hanging around out here all the time."

"Marshal, we're real sorry about that. Truly we are. But Wilse, he told us we're in our lawful rights t' be here."

"Wilse?"

"Wilse is Wilson Yarnell, Marshal. He was with us on the drive up here. He knows a lot, Wilse does. An' he says we got the right."

135

"Where is this Wilse now?"

"He's off seein' if he can find us something to eat or mebbe a bottle, Marshal."

"Seeing if he can *find*?"

Both boys looked embarrassed. Apparently the question touched a nerve. Yarnell was probably off somewhere looking for an opportunity to swipe something. They didn't answer.

"So while this Wilse is away looking for grub and liquor, you two are left here to fight it out with a two-time killer in case he shows up."

The young one squared his jaw and looked Longarm in the eyes. "Yes, sir. That's about the size of it."

Longarm fingered his chin thoughtfully. "Did Mr. Wilse Yarnell mention to you what would likely happen if a gang of killers did come by?"

"A gang of—?"

"Did he mention that everyone is looking for the one fella they can identify but that there are *six* men in that gang?"

"No, but . . ."

"I don't suppose you've thought much about facing six proven killers with guns in their hands?"

"No, but . . ."

"With those toys?"

"We can shoot, damnit, and we ain't scared." It was the older one, and he sounded like he was getting hot now.

Longarm smiled. "I'm sure you can. Quick on the draw, are you?"

The boy frowned.

"Go ahead. Show me."

"Look . . . Marshal . . . we don't . . ."

"Go on, damnit. Show me. Right over there. See that rock on the ground? That should be safe enough in that direction. I'll give a yip, you won't know when, and I want the both of you to drag iron and shoot that rock. It's about the size of a man's head, wouldn't you say?"

The younger one looked a trifle uncomfortable about the idea of the stone being the size and approximate shape of a human head.

"Well?" Longarm demanded.

"We don't want t' waste our ammunition on funnin', Marshal."

"It isn't funning. It's damn well serious. And I'll tell you what else. If either one of you boys can put a bullet within five feet of that rock before I can hit it dead center, why, I'll buy each of you a box of fresh ammunition for those guns you're carrying *and* a sack of groceries."

"Five feet?"

"That's right. Either one of you."

"Marshal, we're pretty good. We practiced the whole way up here, an' everybody said we're good."

Longarm smiled. "In that case, son, you'll have plenty for dinner, won't you?"

"Shee-it," the older one said. "You're serious?"

"I'm serious."

"What if we lose?"

"We'll discuss that if it happens. I won't try and force you to do anything you don't want. I promise you that."

The older one looked at his buddy and grinned. "Marshal, you got you a bet."

At least the boys had sense enough to crawl down off their horses and tie the animals before they went to making noises. Longarm might have objected to that—after all, he wanted to discourage these kids just as thoroughly as possible—except that his livery horse, too, was untrained to gunfire, and the lesson he had in mind wasn't apt to take if the rented horse went and made a joke of it once guns started going off nearby. Longarm dismounted, too, and tied his horse next to theirs.

He walked over to the rock in question and paced off seven steps back toward the boys.

"Why'd you do that?"

"It's about the distance most shootings take place. About where most men feel comfortable with a handgun."

"Oh."

"Ever shoot a man?"

"No, sir."

"It's something should be thought about before you go getting into any fights. Rocks don't shoot back. Men do. And when you shoot a man in the head you tend to get blood and brains all over everything for yards around. But we won't get into that right now. You boys ready?"

"Just a minute." The older boy with the revolver in his pocket reached down and loosened it so it was barely contained inside the cloth. The other one eased the position of his Smith too. Longarm didn't bother to point out to them there would not be time for that if they got into a sudden gunfight. He was hoping they would figure that much out for themselves shortly.

"Since I'm taking part in this it will be fairer if one of you calls the draw," Longarm suggested. "I don't want either of you to think I'm taking an edge for myself."

"I'll do it," the young one said. Longarm suspected he was slightly the quicker of the two and *would* be giving himself a jump on the call.

"Any time you're ready," Longarm said.

The boy looked at his buddy and winked. Both of them dropped into theatrical crouches with their gun hands poised and fingers hooked ready to show this smart-alec deputy marshal just how quick they damn sure were. Both of them were grinning now.

Longarm just stood where he was, posture relaxed and easy. He yawned and reached with his left hand to scratch his ear.

"Now!"

The word was barely off the youngster's lips before

Longarm's big Colt bellowed, and the head-sized rock sprayed lead and stone chips.

The boys blinked.

Neither one of them had yet touched the grips of his gun. Only the one who had called the start signal had yet reached toward his pistol.

"Jesus," the older one whispered.

"Now that I have your attention," Longarm said softly, "let's you and me talk." He smiled at them. "In fact, if you'll listen to me, I have a good idea where you can get yourselves some dinner and pick up some honest work too." He glanced back toward the Circle Y where Pat Vieren was still struggling to get three men's chores done all by himself before Althea had lunch on the table. "And I'll tell you a few stories about what it's really like to face three-to-one odds when the other guys want to kill you." He smiled again.

The younger boy, the "quicker" of them, looked just a little bit sick.

It was a grandstand deal, of course. But Longarm didn't feel the least bit bad about it.

"Willing to listen to what I have to say now?"

"Yes, sir."

"Good." He led the two boys into the shade of the willow stand, gave them each a cheroot and began to talk.

Chapter 28

Downtown Denver was no place for the nuisance of a saddle horse, so Longarm returned the rented animal to the livery and took a train back to the city.

Normally cavalier on the subject of reports and office contact, Longarm this time was feeling he owed it to Billy Vail to keep the boss informed of his whereabouts and progress. Or lack of it.

He reached the Federal Building shortly before noon. As usual, Henry was at his desk in the outer office. The United States marshal's door stood open, though. And Henry looked worried. Longarm greeted the slender, bespectacled clerk with a raised eyebrow.

"You aren't going to believe this, Longarm."

"Mmm?"

"The marshal said he was going to lunch. Early. And that I shouldn't look for him before midafternoon. Or later."

"You're kidding me, right?"

Henry shook his head. "I'm serious. He left nearly an hour ago."

"Billy never does anything like that. Hell, Henry, he works longer hours than you do."

"He isn't acting himself today, Longarm. What's more, he got a telegram this morning. From Washington, but I don't know from who or what it said. He didn't tell me. I know good and well it was official business, but he didn't tell me what it said." Henry sounded aggrieved. Longarm had to admit, though, that it was most unlikely Billy to keep his clerk uniformed about anything that affected the functions of this office. "After the wire came in he moped around here a little while, then got his hat and just . . . left."

"Did he say where he was going?"

Henry shook his head. "Not a clue."

"Brown Palace, maybe?"

Henry shrugged.

Longarm retrieved the brown Stetson he had already hung on an arm of the coat rack.

"If you find him . . . ?"

Longarm stopped in the doorway.

Henry gave the tall deputy a searching look, then frowned and shook his head again. "Nothing, Longarm. I'll . . . hold down the fort here. As long as it takes."

Longarm nodded and left the gloomy office.

Billy Vail was in the last possible place Longarm would ever have expected to find him. In fact, Longarm didn't actually find him. He was pointed in the right direction by a wonderstruck errand boy he ran into at Lambrino's Café. The boy was a part-time employee in the attorney general's office who was an inveterate gossip and a great admirer of Marshal Vail's deputies. He was at the café picking up snacks for several of the lawyers who worked upstairs in the Federal Building when he noticed Longarm and sidled over beside him.

"Hiya, Marshal."

"Hi, Ricky. How's it going?" Longarm didn't want to be impolite to the kid, but by now he was becoming concerned about Billy and was intent on looking at the customers in the café. He peered over Ricky's head while he checked the men at each of the tables in the popular downtown eatery.

"Not so bad, Marshal. Not so bad." Ricky used a thumbnail to pick a bit of leftover lunch out of his teeth and grinned. "Is it true what I heard th'safternoon, Marshal?"

141

"What's that, Ricky?" Longarm was still looking over the customers.

"Heard 'at Marshal Vail got the sack t'day, I did."

The boy had Longarm's full attention now. "Where'd you hear a thing like that, Ricky?"

The boy shifted nervously under Longarm's cold stare. "Well, I didn't so much hear it as figger it, y'see."

"Figure it? How do you *figure* it?" Longarm demanded.

"Well, I mean . . . you know."

"No, I *don't* know, damnit. Tell me."

"Well, I mean, him settin' over there gettin' sloshed an' everything in the middle of a workin' day. An' I just thought . . ."

"Sitting where, Ricky?" Longarm's voice was cold.

The boy blinked. "In th' lounge. Over t' the statehouse. I just come from there, see, an' Marshal Vail, he was . . ."

Longarm was no longer listening. He was out Lambrino's door without a backward look and heading for the basement room beneath the State House of Representatives offices that had become an unofficial and entirely informal club and gathering place for Denver's politically inclined.

It was a place where U.S. Marshal William Vail *never* went.

Except, apparently, today.

"What the fuck are you doin' here?" Longarm demanded. His voice was a low, harsh whisper delivered close to Billy's ear as Longarm bent uninvited into a chair at the marshal's solitary table.

Billy Vail looked at him and smiled. "Care for a drink, Custis?" He reached for one of several wine bottles on the table—the others were empty—and with his other hand motioned for the waiter to bring another glass.

142

"I don't want a goddamn drink. Jeez, Billy. Jeez."
Longarm glanced around the large room. Through a
haze of cigar smoke he could see at least two dozen men
high on the pecking order of the state's government,
nearly all of whom were pointedly ignoring the U.S.
marshal in their midst.

Billy saw where Longarm was looking. He chuckled.
"Oh, by all means, Custis, have a drink with me." He
turned his head slightly so the political hacks would not
notice and gave Longarm a wink.

It was about then that Longarm noticed that despite
all the evidence to the contrary—three empty wine bottles and a fourth partially gone—Billy did not look or
act all that soused.

If anything, he got the impression that the marshal
was rather enjoying this display.

Longarm leaned close and kept his voice low enough
that only the two of them could hear. "Do you know
what you're doing, Billy?"

Vail chuckled again. "Possibly not. Possibly I do not,
old friend. I just, mmm, felt like it."

"And can I ask what the hell 'it' is?"

Billy grinned at him and winked again. "I'm rubbing
their damned noses in it, Custis. Rubbing their damned,
self-serving noses in it."

"Henry said—"

"Henry worries too much."

"He said you got a telegram this morning."

"And so I did," Vail agreed.

"You want to tell me what it was? The, uh, the rumor
is that you been canned, Billy."

Billy Vail threw his head back and laughed loud and
long. But when he spoke it was in a controlled whisper
that would not carry to other ears. "Not yet. Not *quite*
yet. Handwriting on the wall, so to speak, but nothing
formal yet."

"D'you want to tell me who it's from or what it said?"

Vail pondered the question for a moment, then grinned again and shook his head. "No, I don't believe I do, thank you."

"D'you know that you can be one infuriatin' son of a bitch, Marshal?"

"Yes, actually, I do." Billy's grin got wider.

"So fine. Don't tell me. Are we in deeper shit than before, though? Can you tell me that much?"

"Deeper than ever," Billy cheerfully informed him.

"They, whoever the fuck *they* are, still want Big's scalp on a lance or else ours for substitutes?"

Vail grunted and for a brief moment looked serious. "Actually," he said, "I am getting the distinct impression at this point that no one in Washington gives a fat crap about your Mr. Little. Or about the federal employees murdered by Mr. Little and, um, associates."

"What d'you mean?"

Billy gave the room at large a vacant, loose-lipped glance. From any distance at all he must surely look like a midday drunk. At close inspection, though, Longarm could see that the slackness stopped short of Billy's bright, searching eyes. Billy was feeling mean as shit right now, Longarm suspected. But he was not anything close to being drunk. He began to think that perhaps the boss had come here to test some waters and find out just who among the statehouse regulars was lining up against him.

"What I mean," Billy said calmly, "is that I think your Mr. Little is a most convenient excuse for someone to pin my ears to the wall. And yours, of course. Sorry about that, Longarm. I seem to have peeved someone in high places, and you will be going down with me."

"Who?"

"I have no idea"—he smiled grimly—"yet."

"Parkhurst?"

144

"Possibly. Although Leonidas might only be jumping on a bandwagon already set in motion by someone else. It's a little early to tell."

"Damnit, Billy, I wish t' hell I knew more about politics an' politicians. I wish I knew how to help you with this. The only kind of bullshit I know how to deal with, though, is the kind you can scrape off your boots. The kind that goes on upstairs here, well, I just don't know how t' handle that."

Billy poured wine into his glass sloppily and splashed more into the glass brought for Longarm. He knew perfectly good and well that Longarm wouldn't touch the puny stuff, but he made a show of it anyway.

"I have some enemies in high places," Billy admitted. Then with a wink he added, "But I have some friends, too. Don't worry about it. We'll sink or we'll swim, Custis. In the meantime, just go out and do your job. Let me worry about this end of it."

"I just wish . . ."

"I know. And I thank you. But don't worry yourself about it. You concentrate on finding Little and his gang. That's what you do best."

"I just wish I thought it'd be enough."

"Don't be so gloomy, Longarm. That isn't like you. Besides, it could be a help here too. Might take enough wind out of somebody's sails to buy me a little time." Billy saw someone he knew across the room—Longarm didn't recognize the portly fat cat—and saluted him with an uplifted wine glass. The politician pretended not to see the greeting and turned to speak to someone else.

Longarm couldn't see that the brief nonexchange amounted to much, but Billy acted like it had told him something, so maybe it had.

"I wish t' hell . . ."

"Just go out and do your job, Custis," Billy said. "That's all I ask."

Longarm sighed. He left the glass of wine untasted

on the table and got the hell out of there. This was murky damned water as far as he could tell, filled with sharks that a man couldn't see until they already had him by the nuts. It was water, though, that Billy had always been able to navigate before. Longarm hoped to hell the boss still could find his way among these asshole politicians.

Chapter 29

Big Little was the leader of the robbery gang, or at least was the murderous gunman everyone paid attention to. He was far and away the most recognizable one of the six robbers. But, damnit, Longarm couldn't *find* Big Little.

He, everybody, was hellbent on finding Big. With no success whatsoever.

So if they couldn't get a handle on Big, maybe Longarm could find a direction to point toward by inquiring about the rest of the gang.

So far just about all the conversation he'd heard about the post office robbers concentrated on two things: the shootings and the huge, limping man who did the shootings. No one, Longarm included, had paid all that much attention to the other five.

The thing to do, he concluded, was to start fresh on this investigation. Act like he was coming onto it for the first time and start right over again. But this time forget about Big Little and try to get a line on at least one of the other five.

Grab hold of the tail of a rattlesnake and it just naturally follows that you can find—and hack off—the SOB's head too.

Find any one of the robbers and there was a good chance you could bring the whole bunch down.

Longarm's mistake thus far, he decided, was that he'd simply made a bad choice about which robber to chase.

It was a mistake that wasn't too late to correct.

Of the three post offices hit by the gang, Englewood's was the one he had already looked at the most closely. Broomfield's was the furthest away. And Aurora's the most easily accessible from downtown Denver. Longarm hopped a passenger local for Aurora and reached the post office just before quitting time. His search for Billy Vail had occupied most of the afternoon.

"We're about to close up and— Wait a minute. Aren't you one of the marshals that was here before?"

Longarm recognized the postmaster too. Jesse . . . it took him a moment to recall the man's last name . . . Morris. That was it.

"That's right, Mr. Morris. Go ahead and close up. I need to talk to you some."

"If it will help you find Fred's killer, Marshal, you can have all night. Whatever it takes."

Longarm frowned. So the clerk Fred Samson had died. The last Longarm heard the man was still hanging on, although the bullet in his back had penetrated a lung. He was genuinely sorry to hear that the young man died of his wounds and said so.

Morris frowned and nodded. "Terrible thing. Fred was a fine boy. His folks are taking his death awfully hard."

"I'm sure they are," Longarm sympathized.

Morris came around to the lobby area and bolted the door shut, then hung a CLOSED sign in the window. Longarm followed him behind the counter and remained silent there while the postmaster finished counting the day's receipts and locking them, the stamp drawer, and a bag of mail into the safe.

"There doesn't seem to be very much there," he observed once the safe door was shut for the night.

"Oh, there never is, really. All the big business goes through the main post office in Denver," Morris said. "We usually have a few hundred dollars on hand in cash and a few hundred more in stamps."

"Not much in exchange for a man's life, is it."

148

"A pittance," Morris said with a grimace.

"The blank money orders would be worth something, of course," Longarm mused aloud. "Whatever a man wanted, I suppose."

"Not so much as you might think." Morris pointed Longarm toward a chair and settled into one himself. He pulled out a pipe and began to fill it, while Longarm reached for one of his own cheroots. "You see, our money orders are all serial numbered. Just like currency. And naturally I sent out a list of the numbers on the missing money-order forms. Now I don't say that every postmaster in the country will check on the numbers of every money order that's cashed at a U.S. post office, Deputy. But certainly every one of any appreciable size —say, anything over ten dollars—will be checked, at least this side of the Mississippi. We're very careful with money orders. People try to forge inflated amounts on them all the time, so we are routinely cautious of them to begin with. You simply wouldn't believe how common it is for someone to buy a money order for a dollar and then try to convert it to eleven dollars or a hundred and eleven and then cash it."

Longarm nodded. In fact, he would believe it. He'd learned to believe damned near anything when it came to the devious venality of the human race.

"So we are attuned to caution as a matter of habit when it comes to money orders," Morris said. "There were seventeen blank forms stolen in the robbery when Fred was killed. I would say that if the murderers try to cash those for more than ten dollars apiece the numbers are sure to be checked and the forgers apprehended."

"So we're looking at a maximum value of another hundred seventy dollars for the money orders," Longarm said.

"I would say so, yes." Morris's pipe was not drawing well. He retamped the tobacco and lighted it again.

"They got even less than I thought then, Mr. Morris.

I've been assuming right along that a blank money order was worth a helluva lot."

"Not so," Morris said comfortably. "We postmasters are all political appointees, true, but by and large we do our best to be efficient and conscientious in our duties. And there are very strict controls on our cash and stamps and money orders. I daresay it would be more difficult to embezzle from a post office than from any other form of government office."

Longarm grunted. "I take it none of the serial numbers you sent out have come back yet? No reports from anyplace?"

"I certainly would have informed your office if any had," Morris said. "None have been reported. None cashed and none attempted to be cashed."

"The stamps are worth plenty, though."

Morris smiled. "Tell me, Deputy, have you ever tried to pay a bill with postage stamps?"

"Pardon me?"

"Think about it, Deputy. Where can you spend a postage stamp? At a post office, of course. But *only* at a post office. I know that I for one would become extremely suspicious if anyone came in here and tried to convert large amounts of stamps to cash or money orders. The only thing a stamp is good for is mailing a letter or a parcel, really. If someone tried to exchange stamps for cash here I should certainly call our local police and have that individual investigated. So for all practical purposes, the men who murdered young Fred did so for the value of the cash alone, which was only a few hundred dollars."

And only, Longarm realized, a few hundred in actual cash from the Englewood and Broomfield robberies as well. He clenched the end of his cheroot between his teeth and frowned.

Now this was one little thing that he hadn't particularly thought of before.

He, and he suspected everyone else as well, had been

thinking of the reasoning behind the robberies in terms of the loot gained from them. Cash, stamps, money orders and whatever was in the outgoing mailbags taken.

But if the stamps and money orders were as good as valueless to the robbers... His frown deepened. Why the fuck were these robbers so persistent when they got so little?

For that matter, why post offices?

A few hundred bucks in cash split six ways was almighty little.

The same six guys could knock over any saloon on a Sunday morning and get twenty times the money with not a lick more effort.

The gang could rob a stagecoach or a train or a bank, get more money and even avoid breaking any federal law if they were halfway sensible about what they were doing.

So why post offices?

Why were these people doubling their own grief—by having both local and federal peace officers on their butts—and at the same time willfully limiting their take from the robberies?

Longarm asked as much of Postmaster Jesse Morris and got a shake of the head in return.

"I'll be damned if I know, Deputy. I've thought about this and thought about it, and I cannot find a single logical response to that question." He pointed toward the locked front door and the street beyond it. "You could walk right over there to Sol Adams' mercantile and steal three, four, ten times as much money out of his till as you would ever find in my cash drawer. So why did they come in here and murder poor Fred?" He shook his head again. "I simply do not know, sir. I simply do not."

"What about... hell, I don't know. Could someone be trying to steal first-class mail so they could read it and... like learn secrets, something like that? Stock

151

market or livestock market price information? I'm grasping at straws, Mr. Morris. I know that. I'm just trying to understand."

Morris shook his head again. "I wouldn't think so, Deputy. Market quotations or any other information of value is more likely to move by coded telegraph message than by the mails these days. The mail is slow, and—I hate to admit this, but it's true—vulnerable to loss or misplacement. Anything of a timely and valuable nature is much more likely to go by wire than by mail."

Longarm muttered a few curses.

"I wish I could help you, Deputy. I really do. Most of all I wish I could bring poor Fred back. Such a fine young man and dead so uselessly. Such a waste."

Longarm and Jesse Morris talked a while longer. But when Longarm finally left the Aurora post office he was more confused than when he had come.

And just as after the Englewood robbery and killing, when he left he knew absolutely nothing more than he already had about the five men who were Big's partners in the gang.

Jesse Morris's attention had been focused almost entirely on big, flashy Big Little so there was as good as no description available on any of the other men.

Now he not only had no leads on the rest of the gang, even the *motive* for the multiple robberies and killings was falling apart.

The robberies were committed by invisible men and the killings done for little more than pocket change.

This made damned little sense, Longarm realized.

On the surface of it, anyway.

One thing he knew for certain was that it made perfectly logical sense to some-damn-body.

No crime is committed without some reason. Some *good* reason. Good, that is, to the criminal.

Revenge, perhaps? Was the gang led by someone with a hard-on for the post office? A fired postal employee? Perhaps a discharged postmaster? Except, damnit, the gang was being led by Big, and Longarm knew for certain sure that Big was no politically appointed postmaster.

So what the hell *was* the reasoning for knocking over post offices when there were so many other much more lucrative targets virtually next door to the post offices that had been robbed. And why so damned vicious about it if post offices had to be the targets for the gang? Why shoot when there seemed to be so little reason for the violence? Shootings only made pursuit all the more determined. Most professional robbers would pull a trigger only as an absolute last resort measure and would turn themselves inside out to avoid killings if there was any way they could do it and retain their freedom, simply because they were more likely to remain free if they generated no real hatred by killing a posseman's friends. A lawman is always much more determined if a murder is involved, and criminals know it.

So why?

Quick guns. Piss-poor returns. Dangerous targets.

Everything about this case went against the grain of common sense, and the more Longarm learned, the less any of it seemed reasonable to him.

He sat in deep, frowning concentration the whole way back to Denver.

Chapter 30

By first light the next morning Longarm was at the railroad depot. He took the early train to Broomfield and headed immediately for the town's post office. The local police chief, Mason, had told him and Billy that the Broomfield postmaster was a man named Kreiter. Longarm did not recall ever meeting Kreiter but had heard of him. Kreiter held the same positions, both official and unofficial, in Broomfield that Mack Bowen had held in Englewood. That is, the man was a behind-the-scenes power dealer in the local community as well as being a political appointee in the postal service.

The post office was closed when Longarm arrived, even though by then it was 8:35 and the business hours displayed on a sign in the front window said the place should be open already. Longarm tapped lightly on the glass. There was no response so he knocked again, louder this time.

He began to get peeved. Damnit, of course Kreiter would be running behind on things with his clerk recently killed and probably no time yet to find a replacement for the dead Jeckman. But even so he should be inside by now attending to getting ready to open. Longarm banged loudly on the door.

"Hey, you." A man stuck his head out of the store next door to bark at the noisemaker. He first glared at Longarm, then blinked as recognition came. "Say, aren't you . . . ?"

Longarm recognized him too. The storekeeper had been one of the possemen riding with Chief Mason when Longarm and Billy intercepted them in their failed pursuit of the postal robbers. Longarm greeted him and asked, "What time will they be opening here?"

The storekeeper frowned and said, "I don't think they will be open today, Marshal."

"Damn. I haven't got so far off in the days that there's a holiday today, have I?" This wasn't a Sunday, and he couldn't for the life of him think of what national holiday it might be.

The storekeeper frowned again. "You haven't heard?"

"Heard what?"

"I thought . . . I mean I just naturally thought you'd come here to investigate Bernie's murder. I guess you hadn't heard about it."

"Murder? No, damnit, I haven't heard about any murder here except Jim Jeckman's the other day."

The storekeeper shook his head. "Bernie Kreiter was murdered last night."

"But—"

"It wasn't another post office robbery, Marshal. Nothing like that. Just a drunken argument sort of thing, I guess. But I don't really know much about it. Maybe the chief can help you."

Longarm got directions to the police station, which turned out to be a block away in the basement of City Hall, and hustled over there.

He found Aaron Mason behind his desk, looking haggard and baggy eyed from lost sleep. The Broomfield police chief apologized for not reporting the murder to Billy Vail's office. "It's something I was gonna get around to this morning." He sighed. "Along with a bunch of other stuff."

"Mind if I sit down?"

"Oh. Sorry. Sure." The chief motioned Longarm to a chair and rubbed at his face and eyes. He looked like he hadn't slept in quite some time. Longarm offered him a cheroot, which was refused, and lighted one for himself.

"The reason I came up this morning was to talk with the postmaster about the robbery the other day. Now I hear he's dead too," Longarm said.

"I'm sorry to say it, Marshal, but it's true. My jurisdiction, I suppose, since it was a local thing, but if you want to get into it I'd appreciate the help."

Longarm raised an eyebrow and waited for the police chief to explain the circumstances of the postmaster's death. They could worry about jurisdictional questions later, although Longarm probably had authority in the matter simply by virtue of Kreiter's federal office.

"I don't know yet for sure what happened last night," the chief admitted. "I know Bernie spent some time after supper last night drinking at Judith Whist's, um, place of business. Bernie was divorced, you see. No reason he shouldn't be there. No reason at all. He spent some time with a girl called Nelly. I've already talked with her. She says he was his usual self last night. Didn't act like he was worried about anything and didn't have any, uh, trouble taking care of business with her."

Longarm understood what the chief was saying. A man with troubles on his mind but trying to put up a front of normalcy might show his nervousness by not being able to get it up. Not every local lawman would be sharp enough to think about that. Longarm's estimation of Chief Mason's abilities bumped upward.

"Nelly said he was normal as pie an' spent just a little time with her. Then he went back out into the parlor and had a few drinks. You don't know Broomfield so well, Marshal?"

Longarm shook his head. He didn't.

"Well, you should understand that Judith runs a nice, quiet place. Very popular with the better class of gentlemen here. Her place is as close as we've got to a club where the better folks gather. Though some of 'em are married gentlemen and I'd rather not get into names unless you need."

Longarm shrugged. It wasn't the sort of thing he

could decide until he knew more about what happened here last night.

"Yeah, well anyway, Bernie talked with some of the gentlemen and had a couple drinks. It wasn't anything unusual. He stopped at Judith's four, five nights a week. Liked his rest, Bernie did, so he didn't generally stay too late. He'd stay there until nine or nine-thirty of an evening and then go home. Which is what he did last night. No one paid particular attention, mind, but everyone who was there—and I've talked already with everyone who was there, girls and customers too—says it would've been nine or a little after when Bernie said good night and left. Nothing unusual at all."

Longarm nodded and puffed on his cheroot. Chief Mason did not need any prompting.

"Bernie definitely wasn't drunk when he left Judith's place," the chief added. "He'd had one drink before he went to the room with Nelly and two, maybe three after he came back out. Judith said she poured him two drinks that she can recall, but it isn't unusual for a gentleman to help himself to the decanters if he wants. However many drinks he had, everyone agrees that Bernie wasn't drunk when he left. And he wasn't a belligerent sort of man even when he was drunk, which wasn't often at all. Bernie tended to get the giggles instead of putting a mad on when he was in his cups." Mason sighed and rubbed at his eyes again. He must have worked straight through the night to have completed all these interviews by the normal start of business hours.

"Far as I can find, that is the last anyone saw Bernie alive except for whoever killed him," the police chief said. "He was found crumpled in an alley behind Marta Dudec's rooming house about eleven o'clock. The rooming house, by the way, is on a straight line between Judith's place and Bernie's home, so I'm speculating that he was on his way home when he was killed."

Longarm nodded again.

"He was dead when he was found, and the body was cooling but not cold. That'd be consistent with the idea that he was killed shortly after he left Judith's. He was stabbed to death. Stabbed several times in the chest. From the front, so he saw whoever killed him. No broken fingernails or bruises on his hands, so he didn't put up a fight. I don't say this means he necessarily knew the killer, because Bernie was used to people wanting to talk to him about things. I mean, I don't know if you know it, Marshal, but Bernie was what you might call a fixer-upper hereabouts. Politically speaking, that is. He was quiet about it, mostly, but he had a lot o' clout in the places that count. So he was used to people coming to him to ask him favors or pass information along or whatever, and he wouldn't have thought it strange if somebody wanted to talk to him where they wouldn't be seen."

Very much like Mack Bowen in Englewood, Longarm realized. Coincidence? Longarm was not a great believer in coincidence. Coincidence smelled bad, and more often than not there was something rotten at the source of a bad smell.

"So anyway, Bernie was long dead when he was found. Which was just plain luck to begin with. Everybody in the Dudec place was in their rooms and asleep by ten. No one claims to've heard any disturbance outside, though they must have been awake still when the stabbing took place."

"If they were all in bed asleep—"

"I'm getting to that. It was Marta's boy Jimmy that found the body. He told his mama that he was going to the backhouse when he found Bernie. What he told me in private afterward was that he was sneaking out of the house to go visit a ladyfriend." Mason shook his head. "And him only sixteen, too. Damn shame the way the young ones carry on these days. The ladyfriend is in her twenties and married, and I hope you don't want t' know who she is."

"I don't think that'd be necessary," Longarm said quickly.

"Good. We got troubles enough around here without that sorta row getting started." Mason looked miserable. "Two murders, Marshal. Two murders in just a matter of days. That don't seem possible. Broomfield ain't that kinda place. This is a nice, quiet town usually. We aren't used to murders here. Don't want to get used to them neither."

"I don't think you'll need to," Longarm told him.

"You have some ideas about who killed Bernie Kreiter, Marshal?"

"No specifics," Longarm admitted. "Not yet. But I think we're fixing to find out who was behind it. With luck we'll be able to squeeze the details out of him."

It was Mason's turn to raise his eyebrow in inquiry, but Longarm only shook his head. "Too early for names, Chief. I'll get back to you quick as I know something."

Longarm thanked the police chief for his help and left Mason's office without bothering to ask about the gang members who had sided Big Little in the post office robbery, even though that was the question that had brought him here this morning.

It hardly seemed important at this point.

After all, why bother pulling a rattlesnake's fangs when you can chop off the head instead.

Chapter 31

It was not yet noon when Longarm reached the Federal Building. Billy Vail's office door was closed, and Henry was wearing a peevish, worried look.

"Something up, Henry?"

Henry glanced toward the closed door before he answered. "I don't know, Longarm. But I don't like this."

"Who's in there?"

"Deputy assistant attorney general."

"State?"

Henry shook his head. "Justice Department. And two other men I don't know."

Longarm pursed his lips and whistled softly. Obviously the heat on Marshal Vail was reaching an unbearable level.

It was beginning to look like the question was whether Billy would be fired or be allowed the dignity of submitting a resignation.

Fuck 'em, Longarm thought.

He ignored Henry and barged inside Billy's office without knocking.

The men in the room shut up when Longarm came in, but their expressions said the conversation going on in there was not a pleasant one.

The deputy assistant attorney general was a trout-mouthed SOB named Hunter, a newcomer in the office upstairs who had little trial experience and an abrasive manner. With him were a lawyer named Sean Coulter —Longarm knew him to be a penny-ante defense attorney who specialized in getting low-life criminals off on technicalities of the law—and another man Longarm had seen in and around courtrooms but whose name Longarm did not know.

Hunter glared at the intruder. Coulter, Longarm noticed, managed to look both smug and disapproving at the same time. The third man glowered at him.

"What is it, Deputy?" Billy asked. Unlike the others, he did not appear to be particularly unhappy about the interruption.

"I need to see you for a moment, boss."

"All right." Billy remained where he was, standing behind his desk with his hands laced at his back.

"In private?"

Billy frowned. But he turned to his guests and excused himself.

"This better be good," he hissed between clenched teeth as he followed Longarm into the outer office.

Longarm winked at him and reached back inside Billy's private domain to pull the door closed between them and the visitors. He motioned for Henry to join them and led Billy into a far corner. Even then he spoke at a low whisper. Henry's eavesdropping proved that sound carried almighty well inside the U.S. marshal's offices when someone really wanted to listen.

"There's something I got to tell you, boss," Longarm said urgently. "Henry, I'm gonna take Billy with me, and I want you to cover for him. Tell those guys in there . . . shit, I dunno . . . tell them anything." He grinned. "Except the truth, that is."

"Which is?"

Longarm chuckled and motioned Billy Vail and Henry closer so he could speak to them in a soft whisper.

When he was done Billy Vail blinked and stiffened. "Are you sure about this?"

"Hell no, I'm not sure. An' keep your voice down, please. We don't want those, uh, *gentlemen* in there to get their ears to flapping."

"You aren't sure," Billy said.

161

"Nope. But it's the only thing that makes sense."

Billy fingered his chin and pondered the theory Longarm had just laid out. After a moment he nodded. "You could be right. You could also be wrong."

"Shit, Billy, if I'm wrong, I'm wrong. We won't have lost anything anyhow. If I'm wrong it's still a question of when, not whether."

"He's right about that," Henry put in. "I say, do it."

"Just leave? Just . . . disappear?" Billy sounded unsure. But then the idea went against his grain. He was not a man who ran, not from anything, not from anyone. What Longarm was proposing was not the way he handled things.

"Damnit, Billy, you can't make an arrest if you aren't carrying a badge. An' neither can I. If we stay out in the open where those sons o' bitches can find us, there won't either one of us have authority to make arrests."

"Do it," Henry said again. He chuckled. "I can take care of this end of it. Why, I daresay I can lie with the very best of them if I have to. I'll think of something to tell them. Something they can't check up on."

"What about the other men?" Billy protested.

"We can trust them," Henry said. "I'll fill them in, nice and quiet, as they come in. They won't peach. After all, their jobs are at stake too. You go with Longarm, boss. I'll send the other boys out on the sneak behind you. I can think of a few places that might want looking into, just in case Longarm is pointing in the wrong direction with the right idea. I'll put the other boys on those."

"It isn't—" Vail tried to protest.

"Damnit, Billy, *do* it," Longarm hissed.

Reluctantly, Billy nodded.

He stood for a moment looking helplessly around the room. His coat and hat were inside his own office with Hunter and Coulter and the other man.

"Here," Henry said. He grabbed his own derby and

jammed it onto Billy's head, then gave the boss a nudge in the back, sending him toward the corridor in his shirt-sleeves and with an ill-fitting derby perched over his bald dome.

Henry winked and gave them a thumbs-up sign as Longarm escorted Billy Vail into the hallway and out toward the street.

Chapter 32

Billy Vail had been reluctant to begin with, but he warmed to Longarm's theory the more he thought about it. He hired a hansom to take them first to his house and then to Longarm's room.

"I refuse," he told his top deputy, "to be seen in public without a coat and with "—he made a face and rolled his eyes upward toward the narrow brim of Henry's derby—"this *thing* on my head."

At his home Billy changed into clothing that could stand some rough wear and tucked a brace of Colts into shoulder holsters, then left a note for his wife telling her only that he might be out of town for some days and that he would get in touch with her when he could.

At Longarm's room Billy waited impatiently while the tall deputy changed from his usual tweed coat and corduroy trousers into iron-tough jeans and a leather jacket. Longarm retained his vest, however, with its hideout derringer in the place of a watch fob.

Longarm rummaged in his wardrobe for a pair of field glasses before he pronounced himself ready.

"Let's go," Billy said crisply.

Reluctant as he had been to accept Longarm's idea when it was first advanced, the marshal was taking charge now.

Longarm took one last look around the room. He would not dare come back to it now until this business was resolved, one way or another. Nor would Billy Vail be able to go home again until they either caught the mastermind behind the post office killings or both of them were unemployed. Whichever came first.

"After you, boss."

This time they walked instead of hailing a cab. It would be better if there was no hack driver who could tell inquisitive officers where he had taken William Vail and Custis Long.

Longarm slumped against the cold, hard bricks of the chimney, eyes closed and drowsing in a state of half-sleep that was as restful as he could hope for for the time being. Billy was sitting a few feet away on the other side of the chimney with the field glasses.

Despite the discomforts of their situation, the marshal seemed perfectly comfortable and at ease now. It was as if the unexpected call to a field role vitalized him.

Longarm, perhaps because he found this sort of situation more normal, was thoroughly miserable.

This was the second night of their vigil, and Longarm hoped to hell something would break for them soon.

The roof of the apartment building was damned well unpleasant. The night air was chilly enough to be on the brink of being just plain cold, and the chipped, broken slates of the roofing material gouged into his side whenever he tried to stretch out.

They had to be careful, too, to guard against completely relaxing. A bit of inattention, an innocent shifting in sleep, and either one of them could slide off the sloping roof and plummet three stories to the alley below. That wasn't a trip Longarm particularly wanted to make.

Just getting up here after dark was a bitch. Not only did they have to make sure they were not observed, they had to climb a rickety fire ladder two buildings away and make their way across the roofs to get into position.

This would have been a hell of a lot easier, Longarm grumbled silently to himself, if that damned Parkhurst lived out in the suburbs someplace where a man could hide himself comfortably in the bushes at ground level. But no, the son of a bitch had to go and live in an apartment in town so the only way they could keep a watch on him was from a damned roof.

And what if it wasn't Leonidas Parkhurst who was the brain behind the killings?

They hadn't had any contact with Henry since Billy and Longarm slipped away from the political firing squad in the marshal's office. They had no way of knowing if Henry had put any of the other boys on stakeout watching other possible suspects or not.

Still, damnit, Longarm believed it *had* to be Parkhurst. Parkhurst and a number of other greedy, ambitious politicians who wanted to take control of the law enforcement capabilities in the whole damned state of Colorado.

If they managed to do that, if they could get their own puppets appointed to key positions in and around Denver, the SOBs would as good as control the entire state.

That *had* to be the driving force behind the post office robberies, Longarm reasoned. Or more to the point, the post office killings.

The robberies were just so much smoke blowing in the air. It was the killings that made sense.

Otherwise why would anyone risk federal prosecution for a few pennies. That hadn't made any sense at all once Jesse Morris explained the realities to him. So there pretty much had to be something else behind the multiple robberies.

And once he began to get suspicious, a little further inquiry led him to his belief that the whole thing was a matter of politics and not robbery.

Mack Bowen in Englewood was shot dead without reason. Without any *seeming* reason, that is. Now Creel —Longarm hoped one of the other deputies was watching Creel—was the fair-haired boy who expected to inherit control there. And according to Joe Doyle, was going to reshape the Englewood police to his own way of thinking.

In Broomfield, postmaster Bernie Kreiter was dead. No idea yet who would be taking his place, but Longarm was willing to bet there was someone in line for the job. Not necessarily the job of postmaster, particularly, but as the power behind the scenes of political power in the community.

Jim Jeckman's murder must have been a mistake on the part of the gang, a mistake that had been corrected with Kreiter's knifing a few nights ago.

In Aurora it was the postal clerk who was the target of the gang to begin with. The youngster was the only child of Arnold Samson, and Arnold was the man who controlled political patronage in that community. His boy's death shattered Samson. Billy was able to tell him that two-legged coyotes were already lining up to take over from Arnold Samson.

Probably there were other deaths and disruptions being lined up to change the flow of power in other areas too.

Longarm almost had to admire the plan.

By taking out the postal employees, the sons of bitches received the direct benefit of creating vacancies for their puppets *plus* were able to apply pressure to force United States Marshal William Vail out of office.

That would have to be a key part of it, Longarm realized.

Billy Vail and his deputies were *not* for sale, by God, and the people behind this play couldn't afford to allow Vail to remain in office. They had to pry him out of office, too, if their scheme was going to work.

By going after federal appointees like the postmasters first, they would get double benefit from the killings. Create openings for their own people plus give them a chance to grab control of the U.S. marshal's office.

Longarm had no doubt now that someone, probably

Hunter, was already standing in line to take over even from the assistant United States Attorney General in charge of the Denver District. The man now holding that office was as honest as Billy Vail was. So he had to be in line to go soon too. How that one was going to be worked out, well, with luck the plan would never get far enough along for anyone to know.

The only real doubt Longarm had was who was heading the show.

Leonidas Parkhurst was a guess, pure and simple. The best Longarm could come up with but a guess nonetheless.

What he and Billy had to do now was find proof of complicity, any sort of proof, that would allow them to crack the shell of this crowd.

That was why the two of them were in hiding—deliberately avoiding the delegation that would have informed Billy Vail that his services as marshal were terminated—until they could get a handle on the crowd of empire builders who wanted to hold Colorado as a private and corrupt fiefdom.

That was why the two of them had spent the past two nights lurking on a rooftop where they could keep an eye on the comings and goings around Leonidas Parkhurst.

Longarm just hoped to hell it paid off.

"Are you awake, Custis?" Billy whispered.

Longarm's eyes snapped open. "Yeah." He sat up, his shoulders aching and stomach knotting with hunger.

"Four o'clock. Your turn."

Longarm nodded and accepted the field glasses from Billy. He yawned and tried to shake off his fatigue. Billy shuddered and hunched deeper inside his too-light coat, then leaned against the apartment-house chimney and closed his eyes. Longarm knew Billy wouldn't be able to really sleep any more than Longarm could, but at this point a bit of rest was nearly as good as sleep.

"I'll wake you at six," Longarm said.

"Mmm."

Across the alley Longarm could see the dark, blank windows of Leonidas Parkhurst's apartment. That bastard could crawl into bed and sleep as deep and as long as he wanted, damn him.

Longarm swallowed back another yawn and wished to hell he could light a cheroot, but of course there was no way he could show a light on the rooftop over here without giving them both away. Damn that Parkhurst anyway. He cradled the field glasses in his lap and concentrated on staying awake.

Chapter 33

"Billy! Psst! Wake up."

"I'm awake." The marshal sounded alert. More awake, in fact, than Longarm had been feeling until just a few moments ago. "What is it?"

"Parkhurst is up. There's a candle moving through the place toward the front room. What time is it?" All Longarm knew for sure was that it was sometime shy of daybreak. A strange hour, indeed, for a fat cat like Leonidas Parkhurst to be getting up.

"Four-twenty," Billy said.

Longarm was bent forward with the eyepieces of the field glasses pressed to his face. He leaned against the apartment-house chimney to steady them. The field of vision through the glasses was narrow and the light inside Parkhurst's apartment was dim, so he was having difficulty trying to make out the scene across the alley. After a moment he realized he could do better without the glasses.

Parkhurst, he saw, was already up and dressed. Freshly dressed, Longarm knew, because he was wearing a different suit than the one he'd had on the evening before when Longarm and Billy followed him home. The suspect moved purposefully through his rooms, as if answering a knock on the door.

The angle from the next-door rooftop was such that Longarm and Vail could see only the bottom of Parkhurst's apartment door. They were some feet above the level of Parkhurst's floor, so they could only see the man from the knees down when he reached the door.

The door was opened, but Parkhurst remained standing in the doorframe, not inviting his guests inside. Two men stood there. Again, though, Longarm and Vail could only see them from the knees and below. Longarm muttered a curse. He could tell that the early-morning callers were not of Leonidas Parkhurst's class. Parkhurst would have been mortified to be seen in anything less than a suit and tie. The unknown callers wore boots and spurs and soiled jeans.

"What do you think, Custis?"

"Could be something," Longarm ventured.

"Can you make out who they—"

"No, damnit."

"Me neither."

"My gut tells me this could be the fellows we've been waiting for," Longarm said.

"That wouldn't get you far in a court of law, Custis."

"So it's a good thing we aren't in court, right?" On an impulse, Longarm leaned around the chimney and shoved the field glasses into Billy's hands. He stood and started across the roof.

"Where are you going?"

"I'm gonna get down to the ground and follow these birds, Billy. You keep an eye on Parkhurst. If nothing interestin' happens I'll meet you back here tonight or maybe find you sooner outside the Capitol Building." During the past couple days they had developed several locations where they could keep an eye on the state capital building, one of Parkhurst's regular haunts, without being seen. Longarm figured he could find Billy in one of those spots if his hunch about the nocturnal callers didn't pan out.

"All right."

The last Longarm saw of Billy, the marshal was leaning tight against the chimney with the field glasses held to his face and a scowl on his lips.

Longarm hurried to the far end of the roof as quickly as he could without risking a fall on the slippery slate shingles, hesitated only a moment and decided against

171

going all the way to the end of the rooftops at the far end of the block. He had no way to judge how long Leonidas Parkhurst would be in consultation with his late-night callers. And Longarm didn't want to miss them when the pair left Parkhurst's apartment building.

He inched down to the gutter, felt beneath it with a boot heel to locate the downspout and, with a whispered prayer of hope that the spout was solidly attached to the brick wall of the building, lowered himself over the edge.

He grabbed hold of the downspout—an iron fastener creaked and groaned at the intrusion of his weight but did not give way; so far so good—and quickly began to lower himself hand-over-hand down the three-story back wall of the apartment house.

Sounds of snoring reached him through an open bedroom window on the top floor. Sounds of rhythmically creaking bed springs brought a smile of amusement to his lips as he passed the second-story windows. Someone inside knew how to start a day right. The ground-floor bedroom window was closed.

Longarm dropped the last few feet with a grunt of relief, brushed his hands off and dropped into a crouch. He eased silently around the back of the place to the alley that separated it from Parkhurst's building. Far overhead he could see no light now in Parkhurst's windows. If he was too late . . . He hurried quietly on to the front of the building.

He was barely in time to see the two callers emerge.

Longarm looked at them with dawning comprehension. And after a moment a tight, grim smile thinned his lips.

There were two men there, of course.

One of them Longarm was fairly sure he had never seen before. The fellow was tall, six-foot-four or -five, but lightly built. Something of a beanpole of a man wearing a low-crowned hat and a large revolver.

The second man Longarm knew.

172

It was Tom Lee. Pat Vieren's recently fired hand at the Circle Y.

"I'll be go t' hell," Longarm whispered softly to himself.

When the pair set off down the street, Longarm followed behind them in the shadows that were left of the night.

If the two were heading for saddle horses, Longarm decided quickly, he would just have to steal a horse to keep up with them. He could straighten out the misunderstandings afterward.

Chapter 34

Longarm grunted softly to himself. He was satisfied if not actually pleased. But then a man could hardly be pleased about knowing that another murder was being planned.

He'd followed Lee and the tall man to a house on the outskirts of Denver, out past the stockyards. It was broad daylight by now. That would make it more difficult to stay with them without being spotted, but he was sure now that this was the crowd he wanted. Furthermore, he was convinced that they were tending to business. There were six saddle horses tied behind the ramshackle little house Tom Lee and the big man went into.

Six horses handy and six men in the gang Longarm wanted. Thin soup as far as actual evidence went, so probably not enough to justify Longarm taking them here. He would have to stay with them—a shed behind a house a quarter mile away should yield a horse he could steal to keep up with them when they moved— and catch them in the act before they entered the next post office or whatever it was Parkhurst directed them to hit. Whatever political figure it turned out to be that Parkhurst and company wanted killed and permanently out of their way.

Longarm crouched in the shelter of a weed-choked ditch.

Lee and his pal had been inside a good half hour now, and Longarm was debating with himself whether he should go steal that horse now or wait to make sure it was going to be necessary. He decided to wait. Following them on horseback would mean having to give them a long lead anyway to make sure they didn't spot him on their back trail. He didn't have to be in all that big a hurry about getting himself mounted.

A moment later the door of the house opened, and six men filed out.

Tom Lee was with them but did not seem to be leading them.

Big Little was leading them.

He was . . .

Son of a bitch, Longarm realized with a leap of joy.

It wasn't *Big* standing there, *it was the big guy who'd been with Tom Lee at Parkhurst's apartment*.

The tall man was dressed like Big. Like enough to be mistaken for him, anyway. He had on Big's kind of boots and spurs and was wearing Big's kind of high, pinched-crown hat. And where before he'd been a tall beanpole sort of fellow, now he was wearing larger clothes that must have been stuffed with padding of some sort, for his shoulders were large if slightly lumpy.

With a mask over his head even Longarm would mistake him for poor Chester Little.

But now he didn't have a mask on—probably that was what each of them was carrying neatly folded and tucked behind their gun belts—and Longarm could see that it was the man who'd been with Lee, disguised now as the innocent but oh-so-easily recognizable horse lover from the Circle Y.

Of course. Big was so easily recognizable that he was a perfect patsy for these bastards, particularly since the attention of all the witnesses to their crimes would be completely on the mad-dog killer thought to be Big Little. Not only would the disguise point the law's finger at innocent Big, it would prevent anyone from aiming the law at any of the other gang members too.

So Longarm *hadn't* been wrong to ride away from Big that day at the Circle Y.

Now that he thought about it, by damn, he was willing to bet that Tom Lee was the one who scared Big into running away and calling all the more attention to himself when he fled. And it would have been Lee who planted the Navy Colt under Big's mattress for Longarm to find. Hell, it even would've been Lee who tried to ambush Longarm south of Boulder when he rode out from the Sawyer place. Longarm himself had told Lee he was going out there that day. No wonder there'd been an ambush. The gang hadn't been camped in the foothills; Lee'd gone there for the purpose of setting up the ambush while the rest of the bunch hit the Broomfield post office. That was why there'd only been five participating in that robbery. And Longarm's doggedness was probably why Lee got himself fired off the Circle Y, so Longarm wouldn't be around asking him questions about Big so often. That must have made the son of a bitch almighty uncomfortable, although Longarm damn sure hadn't known it at the time. It made sense.

Shee-it! Longarm thought happily.

"Thanks, fellas," he muttered to himself.

Now that the tall man was wearing his Chester Little disguise, there was no longer any need for Longarm to follow and try to catch them in the middle of their next robbery.

Now Longarm had all the reason in the world to march right up and arrest this bunch.

He stood and began walking toward the six, who were chattering quite happily to each other as they snugged the cinches on their saddles.

Chapter 35

"Freeze!"

Longarm smiled at them.

"Or don't." The smile got wider. "Personally, I don't give a shit."

He was standing with the big Thunderer leveled at the tall man's belt buckle.

Up close and without his mask the tall fellow didn't look a thing like Big Little. The illusion would have worked fine, though, if he'd been masked. Hell, he even looked some inches taller than he really was thanks to the high hat crown and the heels of his boots.

"Oh, shit," one of the men moaned.

"Uh-huh," Longarm said agreeably. "That's exactly what you boys went an' stepped in."

The tall one, obviously unlike poor Big in the intelligence department as well as in other ways, began to bluster. "Whoever you are, I—"

"Deputy United States marshal," Longarm said helpfully. "And I happen to be placing all you boys under arrest."

"You have no warrant for our arrest," the tall guy said. "I demand that you—"

"I demand that you fuck off," Longarm snapped. "Now shut up and shuck your iron. All of you."

"You have no right to—"

"You are under arrest. On charges of murder, robbery—I'll think of some more later prob'ly."

"You have no authority to arrest us," the guy returned. "Your badge has been lifted."

"Do tell," Longarm said with a grin. "An' I thought you weren't supposed to know who I am."

The tall man frowned. He looked like he was tempted. Sorely tempted. His fingers twitched, and he looked like he wanted to try for it.

"No limp today," Longarm observed. "You were saving that for later, I suppose."

"You have no proof of—"

"I have enough to take you in," Longarm told him. "Up to you if you walk in or get carried. Makes no difference to me."

"He can't take us all," Tom Lee said. "There's six of us, Marco. He's likely only got five cartridges in that Colt. He can't take all of us." Lee sounded desperate.

Longarm grinned again. "The question, boys, is *which* five of you I kill if you're dumb enough to try me." He glanced at Tom Lee and winked, his grin not wavering in the slightest. "You'll be one for sure, Tom. Payment, you might say, for what you've done to a friend of mine."

Lee blanched and began to tremble. His mouth gaped like a banked fish's. "You wouldn't . . ."

"Try me. Or any of you. Anybody that feels *real* lucky today. But you go down for sure, Tom."

Lee threw his right hand high and with his left scrambled quickly to unbuckle his gun belt and let it fall with a dull thump into the dirt at his feet. "I . . . not me, Longarm . . . not me."

"You?" Longarm asked, locking his eyes on the man standing next to Lee. "How lucky do you feel today, mister?"

The man dropped his eyes away from Longarm's and began to reach for his buckle.

Apparently he wasn't feeling quite that lucky either.

One at a time, Longarm figured. One at a time would be just fine. Because the truth was that Lee'd been right about him not wanting to take six of them on at a time. Damned if he'd show *them* that, though.

While the man beside Lee was tugging at the tongue of his belt, the tall leader of the pack snapped, his tight-wound nerve letting go and driving him into motion.

Marco's hand swept for his holstered Colt while Longarm's attention was on the man beside Lee.

Marco was quick. Longarm had to give him credit.

He wasn't quick enough.

Longarm's Thunderer bellowed before Marco's gun cleared leather, and a thick slug of friction-heated lead smashed into Marco's chest.

The other five scattered like so many quail, several trying to fight but others wanting only escape.

A man with a battered nose and cauliflower ears palmed his Remington and was awarded a bullet in the belly for his troubles.

Another stumbled a few yards away, whirled and spun back around with a gun in hand. Longarm shot him, then missed a snap shot at another man who was in an arm-pumping run toward the stockyards.

The man who'd been trying to get rid of his revolver changed his mind and tried instead to bring it into play.

Longarm shot him, too, a quick bullet taking him in the shoulder and spinning him half around before he slumped to the ground in pain and passed out cold.

Tom Lee was left standing there. He looked pale and frightened. Then his shoulders firmed, and he got hold of himself. He bent toward the gun and belt lying at his feet.

"Tom? You sure you want to try this? You sure you want to die today?"

Lee snickered nastily. "I counted, Longarm. You fired all of 'em. You're empty now. And I don't wanta go back to a cell. I *won't* go back behind bars."

"Been there, have you?"

Lee picked up his gun belt and looked Longarm in the eye. "Yuma," he said. "I won't go back there nor t' Canon City either." He sighed. "You ain't all that bad a fella, Longarm. Pity I can't trust you to keep quiet."

"I fired five, Tom," Longarm said calmly. "So how sure are you that I didn't load a sixth in the cylinder?"

"Man that carries a gun all the time, Longarm, he don't carry all six holes loaded. I know that good as you do."

Longarm smiled. "Even when he knows he's walking into a scrape, Tom? You don't think I'd've loaded the last chamber knowing I was up against six of you?" He grinned. "But you do what you want, Tom. Haul that sucker outa the leather if that's what you believe."

Lee blanched again. He stared down the leveled muzzle of Longarm's Thunderer, then back into Longarm's eyes.

He had his hand wrapped tight on the grips of his Colt. His knuckles were white now, and his hand was trembling. Longarm could see sweat beginning to bead on Lee's upper lip. "I . . . I . . ."

"Go ahead, Tom. Try me, you cocksucker. Try me and *die*," Longarm snarled.

Lee shivered. He looked down the barrel of that dead-steady Thunderer, and he just couldn't do it.

With a groan he opened both hands, his Colt and gun belt both falling to earth again.

Longarm grunted. He pulled out a cheroot and nipped the tip of it off between his teeth, spat the twisted scrap of tobacco out and dug a match from his vest pocket. He lighted the cheroot, puffed on it for a moment and then dipped into the vest pocket a second time to bring his .44 rimfire derringer out. He aimed the little brass gun at Lee and grinned.

"I know this is really gonna fuck up your day, Tom. But the truth is, I was in such a hurry to come put the cuffs on you sons o' bitches that I purely forgot to load that last chamber. I was only carrying five after all."

Tom Lee looked like he wanted to cry.

"Now be a nice fella and turn around, Tom. I need to get you and your wounded buddy there trussed up so I can leave you while I go collect the one that got away.

Then all of us are gonna go back to town and have a long, *long* talk with some friends of mine."

Longarm smiled at the son of a bitch.

Something he was absolutely sure of was that once he got these boys to town at least one of them would begin to talk, trying to save his own ass at the expense of the others.

And if none of them volunteered to open up, why, they could just split them up and lie to them about the others breaking and spilling the beans. Pretty soon there'd be a regular stampede, with each one of them wanting to rush to the head of the line and strike a deal with the prosecutor for state's evidence immunities. And if Longarm had to guess, he would say that Tom Lee was the gentleman most likely to lead the rush.

By nightfall, Longarm judged, there should be one hell of a lot of Denver's finest citizens residing behind bars.

He chuckled. This was the sort of housecleaning a man could enjoy.

Chapter 36

Longarm had a broad grin stretched across his face
when he came into the marshal's office three weeks
later. Henry looked up at him and smiled.

"Have you been over at the courthouse?"

Longarm nodded.

"Well?"

"Come into Billy's office with me. I don't wanta
have to tell it but once."

Henry led the way, knocked lightly on Billy's door
and then let Longarm go inside first.

"Well?" Vail demanded. He looked as eager for the
information as Henry was.

"The grand jury just reported out of closed session,"
Longarm said, relishing the pleasure of the moment.
"They handed down true bill indictments against Parkhurst, Creel, Sid Johnston, Hunter, Coulter—hell,
against the whole crowd of them. Murder, conspiracy,
robbery of the mails . . . you name it."

"It won't hold up," Billy said. "Not against all of
them."

"The least of them will go down for conspiracy and
accessory to murder," Longarm ventured. "Parkhurst
will walk the whole plank. Maybe a couple others too.
That Joyner guy is practically wetting his pants he's so
anxious to get on a stand and testify against them."

Joyner, the one who'd run away and was found later
cowering beside a water trough in the stockyards, had
been promised a sentence of no more than a year in the

182

county jail, no federal penitentiary time, in exchange for his testimony against the rest of the gang.

Tom Lee had tried to strike his own deal, but Longarm had had a quiet word with the deputy U.S. attorney handling the case to make sure Lee was at the back of the line when the deals were handed out.

Lee would go in for at least twenty, and the prosecutor was promising to seek consecutive sentences on the different counts against the man. If that came about, Lee wouldn't ever see another free day in this lifetime.

Longarm felt rather pleased about that prospect.

Billy Vail smiled. "That's good news, Custis." He reached for a telegraph message form on the corner of his desk. "I have some good news for you too. This came in while you were at the courthouse."

"Mmm?"

"The sheriff over in Fremont, Nebraska, followed up on that hunch of yours, Longarm. Big Little showed up at his sister's place day before yesterday." Vail laughed. "You aren't going to believe this, or at least I didn't, but that poor man rode all the way from here to Fremont on that broken-down old horse of Pat Vieren's, bareback, and carrying his filly across his lap. Can you believe that?"

"Knowing Big, yeah, I guess I can. No wonder it took him so long to get there. He would've been as concerned about treating the old gelding easy as he was about not making the filly walk. Lordy, though. He's something, Big is. I hope . . ."

"The sheriff there assures me he's already taken care of letting Little know that he's in no trouble here."

"Damnit, Billy, I want somebody to arrange for Big and his critters to come home. By rail this time. If the department can't pay for it, hell, I'll pay it myself."

"I'm already taking care of it, Longarm," Vail said with pleasure. "The transportation will be courtesy of, um, a group of Denver's finest. If you follow me. Mr. Little and his livestock will travel first class."

Longarm smiled. He followed, all right. There were quite a number of local politicians who should be grateful that they still had their spots at the public trough. Right now there should be favors out there for the asking like leaves on a tree in summertime.

He snapped his fingers.

"Yes?"

"I want to take the rest of the afternoon off, boss. I need to go over to Englewood. There's, uh, a certain party over there who will be glad to hear that Big is on his way home."

"A certain party, huh?"

Longarm grinned.

Vail laughed. "I won't ask you who. I'm sure the certain party is female and probably quite pretty. Am I right?"

Longarm shrugged but couldn't deny it. Sally Anne Hufnagel was concerned about Big the last Longarm spoke to her. She would be glad to hear he was all right.

Very likely she and Longarm would want to celebrate the fact of their friend's safety and impending return.

"Since you're going that way, Longarm, why don't you stop in and tell Pat Vieren, too."

Longarm grinned. "First thing tomorrow morning. After all, boss, I have this afternoon off. Going out to the Circle Y will be an act of official business. So logically I shouldn't have to do it until morning, right?"

"Just don't put an Englewood hotel room on your expense account," Vail said.

"I wouldn't think of it," Longarm assured him.

"And be in the office tomorrow not one minute later than nine o'clock."

"Right, boss," Longarm agreed cheerfully.

With luck, and depending on how late Sally Anne slept in the morning, he *might* make it in by noon.

Watch for

LONGARM AND THE DOOMED WITNESS

one hundred twenty-sixth novel in the bold
LONGARM series from Jove

coming in June!